Also by Dominic Barker published by Catnip
Sharp Beats
Sharp Stuff

Sharp Shot

Dominic Barker

Catnip

CATNIP BOOKS
Published by Catnip Publishing Ltd.
14 Greville Street
London EC1N 8SB

This edition published 2009
1 3 5 7 9 10 8 6 4 2

A CIP catalogue record for this book is available from the British
Library

ISBN 978-1-84647-049-3

Printed in Poland

www.catnippublishing.co.uk

CHAPTER 1

Clocks are liars. They try to tell you that time is always going at the same pace. That one hour in Geography studying soil erosion lasts as long as one hour watching your favourite TV show. It can't be true. One whizzes by and one doesn't. I reckon they've put something in clocks so that they slow down when you're in a lesson. Then at the end of the day they all speed up again. It's probably some kind of government plot to make kids spend all their time in school. That's my theory anyway.

I'm figuring this out because I'm staring at this clock I brought down to my office (well, it's our garden shed really but I call it an office to make myself feel better) and it's going really slowly. It's going really slowly because I'm waiting for a case and I've been waiting for two weeks now. I solved my last one all right. I mean it got me into a bit of trouble but I got the bad guys in the end. And I figured that the word would spread and I'd have people queuing up with

1

cases for me to solve. I even took my ad out of the paper because I was so sure that I'd be in big demand. And what happened? A big fat nothing.

It doesn't seem fair to me. The police never solve all their cases even though they've got cars and computers but people keep going to them, and here's me with a 100 per cent success rate and I can't even get a sniff of action. After a week of nothing I went back to the local paper and put my ad back in – it cost me more money than I made from my last case. I added a couple of extra words this time so they put the price up.

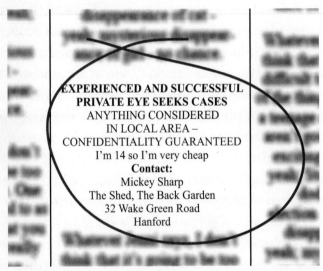

EXPERIENCED AND SUCCESSFUL
PRIVATE EYE SEEKS CASES
ANYTHING CONSIDERED
IN LOCAL AREA –
CONFIDENTIALITY GUARANTEED
I'm 14 so I'm very cheap
Contact:
Mickey Sharp
The Shed, The Back Garden
32 Wake Green Road
Hanford

I thought that putting 'experienced and successful' made it better but I still wasn't sure about the shed bit. I thought about calling it 'the office' because it sounded better but the problem was that if someone came with a case they'd be looking for an office. And they might go away again because all they could see was a shed.

I've tried to make it more convincing though. As well as a desk and a chair and a couple of old boxes I've managed to get a filing cabinet. The people next door were throwing it out. I haven't got any files to put in it and, even if I had, I couldn't because someone locked it and then lost the key. So it's useless but it looks good. Like most pop stars.

And the clock. It's one of those really old-fashioned ones that you wind up. It's been in the guest room in our house for ages. I don't know why we call it the guest room because it's packed out with junk and we never have any guests. Nobody ever uses the clock so I brought it down here. It still works. Old things are like that. They keep working even when everyone's forgotten about them. The trouble with it is that it's got this really loud tick. It puts a big stress on every single second and each tick reminds you that time is passing and you still haven't got a case.

I'm making up my mind whether to let it wind down for the last time when there's a huge bang against the door, which slams it open, and a football bounces in. I watch it bounce. It hits the wall and the bounce turns into a roll. It rolls towards me and stops at my feet.

The clock ticks significantly.

I don't move. Where there's a moving football, there has to be a footballer and I figure that he'll be arriving soon to get his ball back. Five ticks later a tracksuited figure walks into the room and proves me wrong.

'Great goal,' she says. 'You the detective?'

She's not the footballer I imagined. She's got black spiky hair, a nose ring and the best trainers in the shops. She doesn't need to tell me she's an American. I work that out straightaway from her voice. I tell her I'm the detective, all right.

'Sorry about your door. When a girl's gotta shoot, she's gotta shoot. You know what I mean?'

I've got no idea. I nod anyway. I get my pad and pencil out and lean back in my chair. This makes me feel like a detective when I'm on my own. With this girl staring at me through her big dark eyes it doesn't work so well. I stare back at her. I hope it's a good stare.

'It's not like in the movies,' she says.

This shakes me because I thought I looked like I was in a movie.

'This is real life,' I tell her.

'More like pond life,' she says glancing at the corners of the shed, which I've never quite got round to cleaning up.

I can't think of a witty answer straightaway so I

start chewing on my pencil and try not to look too desperate. The silence seems to get me somewhere which doesn't say much for my conversation. She gives this shrug, picks up her football and sits down on a box.

'So what's the case?' I say.

'The case is the problem,' she spits. 'This morning, I went to look at it. And it was gone. I couldn't believe it. I thought it was a joke but it wasn't. Nobody knows nothing about it.' She pulls the football really close to herself like she's guarding it.

'What was gone?' I ask her.

'The trophy, dummy. Haven't I made it clear?'

'Which trophy?'

'The Georgina Best Memorial Trophy for under 12s, stupid.'

'What's that?' I try bravely.

'What's that?' she says.

'I don't know, I just asked you,' I tell her.

She looks like she's going to kill me. But she also looks sexy in a dangerous kind of way. Her eyes look like they've got little bits of fire in them.

'What's your interest?' I say quickly, to distract her. 'You're not twelve.'

'Well spotted, Mr Detective,' she says.

I'm getting the impression she isn't too impressed.

'How old are you?' I ask.

'What does it matter?'

'It could be important,' I say.

'How can it matter that I'm sixteen?'

It matters to me. I'm fourteen and she's sixteen. She might go for younger men, you never know. I just wish I'd started shaving.

'Are you ever gonna ask me a sensible question?'

'Yeah,' I tell her. 'If you're sixteen then why are you interested in a cup for under 12s? You can't win it. Even if you lied about your age they'd spot you.'

She looks confused for a minute and then she reverts to her normal expression, which is kind of fierce. 'Do I look like a soccer player?' she demands.

She's got a tracksuit on, fancy trainers and a ball in her hand. To me it seems like there's only one obvious answer. Still, I have a pretty big feeling that it's going to be wrong. 'Yeah.'

'I'm not a player. I'm the manager.'

'Oh,' I say again.

She seems to be in a big stress about such a little deal. It looks like an easy mistake to make. Even for this angry girl it seems like a bit of an overreaction.

'Didn't you notice this?'

She turns round. On the back of her track suit it says PHOEBE STRADLATER, MANAGER, THE AMAZONS in big letters.

'I'm not too hot at seeing through people,' I tell her.

She turns back to face me.

'I reckon I can see through you. You're no detective. Period.'

As soon as she says 'period' I feel myself start to go red. It's something that happens to me, I don't know why. We have these Personal, Social and Health Education lessons once every two weeks at school with Ms Walter. We did periods last month. Ms Walter said that boys should know about them as well as girls because it was something that all members of society needed to be aware of to promote greater understanding and tolerance. They didn't sound much fun to me. I was as red as a Manchester United shirt by the end of the lesson. We're doing safe sex next week. They give you your own condom. I'm terrified that I won't be able to unroll it. I've never been any good at practical things.

'Why not give me a chance?' I say.

She stares at me and then shakes her head. 'I got no choice,' she says.

'So forget the insults and fill me in. We'll get nowhere if you're just going to stand there abusing me.'

Phoebe opens her mouth to say something else and then she stops herself. It's a big effort. It's like she's choking. She's obviously one of those people who just have to have the last word. She'll probably end up a teacher. They always have to have the last word. In my school it's normally, 'Go and stand outside Mr Walton's office.' He's the Head and he does a good line in shouting and prodding you with his finger whilst telling you that you're a waste of space.

Anyway, Phoebe stops making this choking noise and drags out a booklet thing from her pocket, which she drops on my desk. I give her what's supposed to be a quizzical look. It's something detectives do. They're always doing it on the telly. It's like when you raise one eyebrow as if you're trying to say, 'Aha.' Trouble is that I can't ever get one eyebrow to go up on its own. I've tried it in the bathroom mirror. Both eyebrows go up at the same time and I just look stupid.

I pull the booklet over to me. It says *Rules and Regulations for the Georgina Best Memorial Trophy for Girls. Under 12 section.*

'Turn to rule 18, section 3, subsection 4, paragraph D,' Phoebe says.

I do as I'm told.

'What does it say?' she demands.

I have to kind of squint to read it because the writing is really small, like on those amazing free offers they're always giving you at fast-food places that claim you can win a million pounds in big flashy letters and then right at the bottom in microscopic boring letters it says *only Martians are allowed to win* or something. Competitions like that always have a catch.

Anyway, I read it out,

'Following the satisfactory completion of the tournament when the winner has been determined by the aforementioned rules the trophy will be presented to the captain of the victorious team. The trophy then becomes the property of the victorious team until the completion of the subsequent tournament. It is the responsibility of the victorious team to maintain the trophy in good condition by regular dusting and polishing with approved substances (see list of approved substances in Appendix 3). Upon the completion of the subsequent tournament the victorious team must present the trophy to their successors who will then bear responsibility for it. Should the victorious team be unable to return the trophy they will be disqualified from any tournaments they have entered or attempt to enter in the future.'

'What?' I say when I've finished reading it. It's made about as much sense to me as the past tense in French.

'Isn't it obvious?' she says.

'No,' I tell her.

'The Amazons won the trophy last year in my first year as manager. We've got an even better team this year. We're the best team in the cup. We've got through to the final again. We'd be the first team ever to win the Georgina Best Trophy twice. The final is in three days and the trophy's vanished which means we'll get disqualified and the Blondel Babes will win the trophy automatically. Now do you get it?'

I get it.

'We've got to get that trophy back. We can't let the Blondel Babes win. They wear lipstick during their matches. That's not soccer.'

I don't really get the bit about the lipstick but I understand everything else. I've got to find a trophy. 'You've got a picture of the trophy?' I ask.

She shakes her head. 'No, but you can't miss it. It's black.'

'Black?'

Trophies shouldn't be black. Trophies should be silver. It's like a law or something.

'The guy who set it up did it for his daughter. She'd just died and she loved football and he was sad. So he made the trophy black to show how sad he was.'

Fair enough. 'You got any idea who took it?'

'The Babes took it. It's obvious isn't it? They knew we were better than them and they couldn't bear to lose. They found out about Rule 18, section 3, subsection 4, paragraph D and they decided to cheat their way to the cup.'

'It could have been someone else,' I say. 'Some thief could have stolen it to sell.'

'It's worth about fifteen dollars,' she says.

'Dollars?' I say.

'I always think in American when I'm angry. Ten pounds.'

'How about a stupid thief?'

'It was the Babes, dummy.'

'OK,' I say. 'Where was it taken from?'

'From our clubhouse.'

I tell her I'll need to see the crime scene. Detectives have to see the crime scene on the TV. There's always a clue there that nobody else has noticed. It might be something really tiny but it gives them a lead and from that lead there comes a trail and from that trail they find the crook and before you know it there's a car chase, a big fight and the crooks are wearing handcuffs. All from a little clue.

She looks quite impressed when I say crime scene. So, I go for the difficult bit straightaway. I make my voice sound as confident as possible.

'I charge ten pounds a day plus expenses.'

'No win, no fee,' she says.

'What?' I say.

'No win, no fee. It's standard practice in the States.'

She offers me her hand. I shake it. I decide not to ask her what it means. She gives me the address of the clubhouse and we agree to meet there the next day.

'You better solve this, Mickey,' she says. 'Period.'

She walks out and I feel myself going red again.

This is going to be one hell of a case if I don't get her to stop saying that.

And then almost immediately, the shed door opens and a tiny little lad walks in. He can't be more than six. He's so young he's still wearing short trousers. Short trousers are definite proof that adults don't care about children. Nobody likes wearing short trousers apart from for playing football but adults put kids in them for as long as they can get away with. Why? Because it's cheap. Short trousers have less material in, don't they? But the short trousers aren't the weirdest thing about him. He's wearing glasses and one lens of the glasses has got a patch on it. He looks like a cross between a scientist and a pirate.

'Are you the detective?' he says. Well, he doesn't really say it. It's more like he eaks it. He's one of these kids with really high voices.

I nod.

'I'm Jeremy Thomas and I've got a case for you.'

Typical. You don't get a case for ages and then two come along at once.

'What is it?' I ask.

'My cat has disappeared,' he says.

'Oh,' I say. I can't say I put much interest into the 'Oh'. If it's a choice between finding a stolen trophy for a sexy sixteen-year-old girl and looking up trees for a lost cat for a weird-looking six-year-old lad guess which one I'm going for.

'I've brought a picture of Pudding and here's my address. She was last seen going through our cat flap three days ago. I expect you'll want to get looking right away.'

He talks like an adult. It's just a shame about the squeaky voice. He drops these things onto my desk and then turns round and marches out of the shed.

'Hey,' I shout. 'I can't take your case. I've got other things …'

But it's no use. He's gone.

CHAPTER 2

'Have you seen the colour of the hands this boy's brought to the dinner table?'

It doesn't take much working out to realize that the boy my father's referring to is me.

'Oh, Mickey,' screeches my sister, Karen. She's really overdoing it. It's not like they're covered in blood or anything.

'They're filthy,' agrees my mother.

I look at my hands. All right, they've got a bit of dirt on, but you can't help it in that shed.

'Go and wash your hands,' says my dad.

I go. I don't see the point in people moaning on if you've got a little bit of dirt on your hands. I thought that's why we invented knives and forks, so that we didn't have to worry too much if our hands were clean. Still, that's just my dad these days. All he cares about is finding something to get at me about. If it wasn't dirty hands, it would be something else – he'd probably tell me off for breathing wrong. It's like he hates me half

14

the time. My mum says he'll be better if he gets a job (she used to say *when* he gets one) but even she doesn't look like she believes it any more.

I don't want to think about my dad so I try and concentrate on the case while the tap's running. Would one girls' team nick another team's trophy just to cheat their way to a title? It wasn't like it was the World Cup or anything. I couldn't see it somehow.

'How long does it take you to wash your hands?' he starts off as soon as I get back downstairs. 'I know you don't do it very often and so you're probably a little shaky on the proceedings but I would have thought even someone of your limited intelligence would have managed to work it out.'

It's salad again. My mum and sister have almost finished theirs. This will give my dad a chance to have another go at me for spoiling a family meal. My mum saves me though. She's only got about one forkful left but she keeps pushing it round her plate for the next ten minutes to make it look like she hasn't finished.

I hate salad. We're always having it at the moment because Karen says it's really healthy and low in calories and good for your skin. She's doing Food Technology for GCSE so she thinks she can tell us what to do. She says that we all have to eat more salad and fresh things. Nobody wanted to but she stopped eating for about three days and then my mum started making it all the time. Karen will hardly ever eat normal food any more. It's because she wants to be a model and you're supposed to be really skinny. She hasn't got a chance. She looks so miserable all the time that the only people who'd want to buy clothes they'd seen her wearing would be suicide risks.

The thing about salad is however much everyone tells you it's good for you and fresh and will make you live longer, it's still horrible. Eating lettuce is like eating soggy green toilet paper and cucumber is just water with a green ring round it. Bite into a tomato and inside it's just like spit with seeds in. If we were meant to eat salad, God would never have invented chips.

Not that anybody would listen to me about food. My dad's always telling me that my table manners are disgraceful and my mum just nods when I say anything and then ignores it afterwards. And if I start talking about chips to my sister she just holds her hand up and says, 'Don't go there.' She watches all those American talk shows with fat people who hate each other.

We all work away over our knives and forks, heads down. Beside me, I can feel my dad working up to blaming me for the silence so I figure I'll try to head him off with a question.

'If you stole a trophy, where would you hide it?'

'What?' snaps my dad.

16

'What do you mean?' says my mum suspiciously.

'Suppose that …' I start off.

'If you're in trouble I want to know right now,' says my dad firmly.

'What?' I say.

'Don't "what" me, young man. If you've stolen something, I want to know straightaway. No beating about the bush. Own up to it like a man.'

'Own up?'

'I knew it would come to this.' He stares at my mum. 'Your son, a thief.' He always says that I'm my mum's kid when he's angry with me which is all the time.

'I'm not a …'

'Don't interrupt me.'

'I'm not a thief. It's just for a case.' I say this at about a hundred miles an hour to get it in before he yells at me again.

It stops him for a second but only a second. He's got a new line of abuse in reserve. Who am I kidding? He's got a million lines of abuse in reserve. He's a parent.

'You've still got this stupid detective business going on?' he says. 'I thought you'd grow out of that. Playing silly games. You're fifteen now.'

'Fourteen,' I tell him. He always says I'm older than I am when he wants me to do something responsible. If he wants to stop me doing something he says I'm too young. If I'd asked to stay out late he'd have said it was much too late for a thirteen-year-old. He'd really believe I was thirteen too. He's a bit mad.

'Don't correct me. You're fourteen now, like I said. You should be settling down to some serious school work, not messing around playing at being a detective.'

There's a silence after that. My sister excuses herself to go to the toilet. My mum piles up the dishes and takes them out to the kitchen. I keep very still and very quiet. I'm like those animals you see on the TV sometimes. They're really near some other animal – like a lion – that will eat them but they can't get away. So they stand completely still and hope that the lion thinks they're just part of the scenery.

After a while my father snorts and then stands up and leaves the table. It must be less nerve-racking having dinner with a roomful of mass murderers than it is with my family. At least there's a chance they might pick on each other.

'Your father's under a bit of stress today.' My mum's back from the kitchen. 'He had a bit of bad news in the post this morning and he's been on edge.'

My dad got sacked last year. He can't get a new job. He can't even get an interview. We're all supposed to feel sorry for him. He's forty-nine and nobody wants to employ him. So he shouts at me. It's not my fault. I'd give him a job if I had one. Preferably in Australia.

'Where would you hide a trophy, Mum?'

'I'm tired, Mickey.' She takes the rest of the dishes through to the kitchen to wash them up.

Nobody's any use in my family. I walk off to my room to get a packet of crisps to fill me up after that pathetic tea. I'll never get to be a decent height if I have to try and grow on salad. As I walk past the toilet I hear my sister being sick. I know just how she feels.

CHAPTER 3

'Earth calling. Come in, Mr Sharp, your time is up.'

I'm kicking things around my brain trying to figure out how to solve this case. What if there isn't some kind of clue at the clubhouse? I know there's always a clue on the TV but real life isn't like that. On TV everybody's always fighting and shouting and sleeping with each other and then it all ends happily ever after. In real life people just moan at you and then moan at you some more and then it's bedtime.

'Mickey, for the one hundredth time …' It's Mr Barlow, my Maths teacher, which isn't that surprising because I'm sitting in a Maths lesson.

I ask him, 'What?' and he says, 'What, *sir*?' and I say, 'What, sir?' to make him feel better.

'Where's your homework?'

He's got me there. I know where my homework is. It's in an imaginary world living happily ever after with my dad's good temper and my sister's brain.

'What homework?'

'The homework that was due in last week.'

There's a big 'aaah' from the morons at the back when he says that. The morons love it when someone else is in trouble. They try and wind the teacher up until he gives you a detention or something. They're so thick the teachers don't bother giving them homework. If they spell their names right our English teacher says they're making progress.

'That homework.'

'Yes, that homework.'

'Was it about percentages?'

I just make that up. When in trouble always try to confuse things.

'No, it was the ten equations.'

'Oh, the *equations*.' I say it as if they're my best friends and we're always hanging out together. 'The ones with x and y in them.' Equations always have x and y in them. I don't know why. I think it must be the guy who invented Maths learnt his alphabet back to front which shows you that he can't have been that clever.

'You are trying my patience, Mr Sharp.'

I pick up my bag and start to look in it like I'm looking for the homework.

'I'm waiting.'

I put my head deeper into my bag which isn't a very nice experience. Sometimes I forget to take my PE kit out for a couple of days and the smell sort of lingers.

I once left it in there over the summer holidays and it grew mould. My mum didn't believe me when I told her it was a science project either.

'Why don't you just own up and stop wasting my time?'

Never ever fall for that one. They always tell you you'll feel better if you own up. It's rubbish. They're the people who'll feel better because they can shout at you and give you a detention and do that big speech that teachers just love about how you're wasting your chances and how you may not appreciate it now but one day you'll look back on the time you wasted at school and regret it. You never see a teacher happier than when they're telling you that you'll regret something in the future, 'when it's too late to do anything about it'. I don't buy it though. Who are the people who did well at school? People with loads of qualifications and initials after their names, and what happens to them? Loads of them become teachers. And do teachers look happy? No. They look miserable. They've got lousy clothes and dodgy old cars and thirty kids ignoring everything they say. If that's what qualifications get you, I don't want them.

'Get your head out of that bag.'

I must look like I'm trying to tunnel out.

'Mickey's not got his homework,' scream the morons at the back.

'Give him a detention.'

'Send him to Mr Walton.'

Mr Barlow yells at the morons to shut up. The idea's a bit difficult for them at first but when Barlow's yelled it three times more they just about catch on.

Then Barlow starts tutting and shaking his head. 'What has happened to you?' he sighs. 'I remember you in Year Seven. A lovely boy you were to teach then. I remember telling your mother at parents' evening that you were a pleasure to teach. There was a big smile on her face when she left that evening. This year I suppose she'll go home in tears.'

This is really low teacher stuff when they start reminding you what you were like when you were a little kid. They know everybody will laugh at you and they don't care.

'Well, Mickey. As a punishment you can …'

WAAA-OOH-WAAA-OOH-WAAA-OOH-WAAA-OOH!

The great thing about going to a lousy school is that there's always some fool setting off the fire alarm. Everybody in our class cheers and starts putting their coats on and heading for the door led by Umair. He used to be my best friend but now he sits at the front.

'Now, just slow down,' yells Mr Barlow.

He's got no chance.

'We're all gonna die,' shouts someone.

'I can see flames,' screams somebody else.

'There's the fire brigade.'

'Run.'

The class charge out of the room with Mr Barlow running after them shouting, 'Walk in a straight line on the left and go directly to the emergency assembly point,' even though he knows that everyone will screech out of the school at a hundred miles an hour, run onto the field and start playing football.

I'm left alone so I take my time putting my coat on and doing up my bag before wandering out. There's about as much chance of this being a real fire as there is of the presenters on children's TV not smiling all the time. I remember this old fairytale we read in primary school. This kid Peter gets sent up the mountain by his grandfather to look after his sheep. He gets bored looking after the sheep so he starts shouting, 'There's a wolf. There's a wolf. Help! Help!' and so all the people from the village come up the hill to save Peter and the sheep from the wolf. But the wolf isn't there. Peter's just made up the wolf being there so he says it's run away and then all the people go down the mountain again. Peter likes playing this trick so he does it again and again and again and every time the people from the village come charging up the mountain ready to kill the wolf. They must be a pretty fit village by now if they keep running up mountains but I don't think

24

any of them can have been that brainy because they fall for this trick loads and loads of times. Finally, one of the slightly less stupid people cottons on that Peter might just be lying and all the other people in the village agree, mainly, I reckon, because they're sick and tired of running up mountains. So the next time Peter screams, 'There's a wolf. There's a wolf. Help! Help!', the villagers ignore him. The only problem is that this time there is a wolf and Peter gets eaten. Our primary teacher reckoned that this taught Peter a very valuable lesson. I don't get that. I mean I don't think anybody thinks, 'Wow I've learnt a really valuable lesson', when a wolf is chomping into them, they just think, 'Ow! Stop biting my legs' or something. Anyway, she said the lesson was, 'Don't play tricks on people', which shows that I was wrong because I thought it was, 'Always say no if your grandad asks you to look after his sheep'.

But that's what our school would be like if there was ever a real fire. We'd be like all the villagers going, 'Oh it's just a false alarm.' Imagine being burnt to death whilst doing French. Your last thought would be something like, '*Où est ma mère? Ma mère est dans le jardin.*' What a horrible way to die.

So, everybody has gone by now. I decide I'd better follow them down. Mr Newman, my form teacher, isn't exactly the toughest teacher in the world but he tries his best and sooner or later he's going to get everyone lined up on the playground so he can check off the register and I'll be in more trouble if I'm not there.

I head down the stairs and along the corridor towards the door nearest the playground. Suddenly, I stop. You know when something just flicks past your eye which might just be interesting but your brain doesn't quite register it straightaway. That's just happened to me. I back up. Stuck on the wall there's a piece of paper. It says:

JOIN THE BLONDEL BABES
THE BEST GIRLS' FOOTBALL TEAM
IN HANFORD
ARE YOU UNDER 12?
THEN CONTACT

'*Sharp!*'

My head shoots away from the poster. There are some teachers who can shout and there are some teachers who can really shout and then there is Walton. He's the Head at our school. Shouting is the only thing he can do but he can do it very well. I reckon when they need a new Head at a school they just line up all the people who want the job and the one who can shout the loudest gets it.

'What are you doing, boy?'

'Nothing, sir.'

'Exactly, exactly. You are doing nothing. What should you be doing?'

'Going to the playground.'

'You should be evacuating the building. You should be heading for the nearest exit in an orderly fashion. You should be assembling at the appropriate muster point.'

I go to move past him towards the door. His hand reaches out and grabs me.

'Where are you going?'

'I'm evacuating, sir,' I tell him.

'Sharp, you do not just walk off when a teacher is talking to you. You wait to be dismissed.'

'But there's a fire, sir.'

'Of course there isn't a fire, sonny. Where's your tie?'

'In my bag, sir.'

'It shouldn't be in your bag. It should be round your neck. Put it on.'

This is typical of Walton. He pretends that he cares for kids, he's always going on about it at assembly, but really he just cares about whether you've got your tie on or not. I think he'd rather have dead children in proper uniform with their shirts tucked in than live children with their shirts out.

I put my bag down on the floor, take my tie out and start to put it on.

'Do you realize how long I've spent in education, Sharp?

Thirty years. I'll be eligible for retirement in another two and if you think I'm going to let someone like you mess up my pension by getting themselves needlessly killed whilst in my care you've got another think coming. Because they won't blame you, Sharp. Oh no. You'll be an innocent victim and they'll plant a tree to remember you by. It'll be me that ends up on *Newsnight* being grilled by Jeremy Paxman. But do you ever think about that? No you don't.'

He's right there.

'No consideration for others. That's the youth of today.'

I nod. With teachers like Walton it's just best to agree with whatever rubbish they come out with. He's been teaching so long he's no longer human. You see that with teachers all the time. They start off being a bit human but every year they get more and more like robots. I bet Walton tells people to stop chewing in his sleep.

'Detention with me after school today,' he says.

This is what I've been praying won't happen. I've got to meet Phoebe after school to check over the crime scene.

'You've gotta give me twenty-four hours notice,' I tell him.

They do. It's the law. At least that's what everybody says but I've never seen it written down.

'Sharp, last time I spoke to your father he informed me that I could keep you in school for a week at a time without notifying him and he would pay me if I did. Outside my office at 3.45, please. Now get to the playground. What's that on the wall?'

He walks over to where the Blondel Babes poster is, rips it off and scrumples it up. Just my luck. I never did see who to contact. It's my first lead. I can't let it just disappear. I cough.

'Get to the playground, Sharp.'

I try and make my voice sound pleasant.

'Could I have that piece of paper, sir?'

'No.'

'Please, sir.'

'I've said no.'

'It's very important, sir.'

'No. No. No.'

He tears it up into little pieces in front of me and throws them onto the floor. The fire alarm stops ringing. There's a silence which lasts a second but feels like it lasts for ever. He looks at me and then at the floor.

'Now see what you've made me do. I'm dropping litter in my own school.'

I figure that it's time to get out of there. Walton talks about people who drop litter in assemblies and he make them sound as bad as murderers. If I've got him to the state where he's throwing paper everywhere he's not far from killing me.

'You should pick that up, sir. It's a fire hazard,' I tell him.

And then I run.

CHAPTER 4

There are choices in life. You can watch TV or you can do your homework. You can eat salad or you can eat chips. You can go to detention with a grumpy old man with dodgy breath or you can go to a meeting with a fierce but attractive sixteen-year-old American girl. The thing is, all the things you want to do turn out to be wrong. What a great world it would be if your parents said to you, 'Well done, son, you've spent another whole evening watching the telly', or your teachers said, 'Congratulations, the stuff I've been teaching you in the last lesson was utterly boring and useless and so you correctly spent the time secretly listening to your mp3 player.' It's not going to happen. People tell you off for doing things you like and only praise you for doing things you hate. And then they say, 'You'll thank me for it when you're older.' How do they know? It's not like they're Mystic Meg.

I decide that sitting in a classroom with Walton for half an hour isn't that appealing a prospect so I get on my bike and head down to the football ground to meet Phoebe. I hope I can combine solving the case with encouraging her to show a more sympathetic approach to Anglo-American relations, maybe by indulging in some close contact with a young English detective. I asked my mum once what girls like to talk about and she said, 'Normal things.' What kind of use is an answer like that?

When I get there, it's one of those sad old football grounds which don't have any seats, just a kind of white barrier running all the way round the pitch which people lean on. It's used by loads of different local clubs so there isn't really any grass left on the field. It's just mud with a few white lines on. And the white lines aren't straight.

On the far side is the clubhouse, which is where I'm supposed to meet Phoebe. I see someone standing by the door and head over. It looks pretty secure with mesh on all the windows so nobody got in that way.

Surprisingly, the figure turns out to be a boy. He's about my age. It's a bit weird but, as I get nearer to him, I get this feeling that he's talking to himself. He's dressed really oddly too. He's got this long thick coat on and it's not even very cold. He nods at me. I keep my distance. He's definitely talking to himself.

'Do you know a girl called Phoebe?' I say.

'Sixteen-year-old American manager of the Amazons,' he replies.

'Yeah,' I say.

'One-time player for the Amazons. A dynamic midfielder with a cultured left foot,' he continues.

'What?' I say.

'An inspirational leader who has turned the fortunes of this club around with her tactical insight and radical squad rotation system.'

I haven't the faintest idea what he's talking about. I just stare at him.

'She couldn't come,' he tells me. 'She's been faced with a sudden injury crisis. She sent me instead. Are you Mickey Sharp?'

I nod.

'Novice detective with little or no experience at this high level of competition.'

This isn't the most flattering description of me but I nod again. If this kid talks like this all the time then he's going to get into a lot of fights.

'Follow me.'

I follow him into the clubhouse. It's basically three rooms. At the back are the two changing rooms which are marked HOM and AWA. At the front there's the TROPHY ROOM. It sounds impressive but when you go in, it isn't. The mesh outside makes the room really dark. There are three chairs and a table. And there's a glass cabinet with loads of trophies and shields and a big hole in it. There's broken glass on the floor.

I stand there thinking. The trouble is that I've never really been to a crime scene before and I'm not absolutely sure what to do.

'Sharp seems confused. He stands in the centre of the room in an agony of indecision.'

This is said by the kid who's followed me into the room.

'What's your name?' I ask.

'Clive,' he says.

'Well, Clive,' I tell him, 'I'm thinking at the moment. It may be something you don't see very often.'

'I can only report what I see,' he says.

I decide not to continue the argument. It's not going to get me anywhere arguing with a mad kid.

'Do you want the key to the cabinet?'

I take it and walk over to the trophy cabinet trying not to stand on the broken glass. I put the key in the lock and turn. I'm about to pull the door open when I remember my gloves. They always wear gloves on the TV to avoid ruining any fingerprints that might be there from the crime. I can't actually get any fingerprints because I don't know how but I figure if I wear gloves I'll look like I know what I'm doing. The only trouble is that on TV they've got these see-through plastic gloves and the only pair I could find were a pair of my mum's old fleecy mittens. I put them on anyway.

'Sharp pulls open the door after placing two glove puppets on his hands,' comes Clive's voice from behind me.

'Stop saying what I'm doing,' I tell him. 'And they're not glove puppets, they're fleecy mittens.' As soon as I say 'fleecy mittens' I realize it's a mistake. It's one of those things that you just can't say in a tough way.

'Sharp gets distracted and loses his temper,' says Clive, with a smug smile.

'If you don't want your next sentence to be "Sharp throws Clive through window" then you'd better stop it,' I tell him. I'm bluffing. The windows have got mesh on and he'd just bounce off.

'I'm only commentating,' he says.

'What?' I say.

'Commentating. It's my job. I'm the Amazons' official football commentator.'

He is mad.

'Clive,' I point out, 'this may come as a bit of a shock to you but I'm not playing football.'

'I know,' he says.

'Then why are you commentating on me?'

'Practice,' he says. 'Footballers have to train and I have to practise. It's going to be tough to get a job on

35

Match of the Day and I've got to practise all the time. I commentate on everything.'

'Everything?'

'Everything.'

I'd hate to be there when he goes to the toilet.

I turn back to the cabinet. The thing is jammed full of cups and shields but I don't need more than a quick glance to see that there's no black trophy. I pick a few up to see if anything's fallen behind them. There's nothing except a few bits of glass. I scan the floor. I don't see anything. I examine the chairs. Down the sides and underneath. Nothing. I check the table. I check under the table. There still isn't a clue. It isn't fair. There's always a clue.

CHAPTER 5

'Hey, Freakshow. Who's this?'

I look up. Standing in the doorway is a boy. He's about sixteen. He's got blond hair and a suntan. He's only wearing a towel and there's a gold chain round his neck. He must have just come out of the shower because there's still water dripping off bits of him. He's got a bottle of gel and he's rubbing loads of it into his hair.

'On the floor,' says Clive, 'we have a new recruit to the backroom team of the Amazons. Mickey Sharp, teenage detective.'

'What's he doing on the floor, Freakshow?'

You know when you don't like someone straightaway. Well, multiply that feeling by about a thousand and you get what I feel when I look up at this guy. I don't like the silly smile he has on his face as he looks down at me. I don't like the way he talks about me like I'm some kind of worm and I don't like the way he calls Clive 'Freakshow'. I mean Clive's obviously mad but that doesn't mean you should call him 'Freakshow' to his face.

'Sharp is investigating the crime scene.'

'Why's he got mittens on, Freakshow?'

I knew the mittens were a mistake.

'Look, excuse me,' I say. 'This crime scene is closed. Can you leave, please?'

He starts laughing. He's got one of those big stupid laughs that don't sound real. It's like the ones you hear chat-show hosts do when one of their guests tells some story they don't think is funny but they've got to laugh anyway.

'Did I hear right, Freakshow? Did I hear right? Is he asking Kyle, Kyle Kingston, The Kylester to leave the room?'

'The detective did seem to say that,' says Clive, 'even though there is no video replay to establish whether that was precisely what he said. It will certainly be a talking point later on.'

'Does he know who I am, Freakshow?' says Kyle. 'Does he know that I am Kyle Kingston?'

'I know you're Kyle Kingston,' I tell him. 'You've said it often enough.'

'But does he know what Kyle Kingston means?'

The way he talks to me without talking to me is really annoying.

'Does he know that Kyle Kingston is the best

footballer in the local area? Does he know that Kyle has had four Premier League teams begging for his signature? Does he know that the KK scored on his debut for England Schools in their three-nil victory over Welsh Schools? Does he know that The Kylester has a list of girls begging to go out with him, all of them so sexy that they have been offered modelling contracts? Does he know, Freakshow? Does he?'

'I know,' I tell him. 'Nice meeting you. Goodbye.'

He doesn't go anywhere. Instead he breathes in hard, puffs out his muscles and stares at me.

This is one of those situations that being a teenage boy you get in every now and then. It just happens. One guy wants one thing, another guy wants another thing. Neither of them backs down. They stare at each other a bit and then someone ends up getting hit in the face. I look at Kyle and I think about me and I know that I'm the one who's going to get hit in the face.

I shrug. It's a shrug that's meant to say if you want to be so stupid about it then I suppose I'll have to let you. But it's also a shrug that says that I'm not going to fight him. It's something you have to do now and then to get yourself through life without too much damage. Guys who don't learn to shrug are going to get put in hospital sooner or later. It's probability. We did it in Maths.

'OK, Sherlock. You know it makes sense not to argue with the Big K.'

He's not one of those guys who make shrugging very easy.

'It's about the stolen trophy, right. Kyle talked with Phoebe about it. The Kylester is very helpful to Phoebe in a number of areas and we ain't just talking tactical formations if you catch my drift.'

I catch his drift all right but it's the kind of drift I don't want hanging around inside my head so I try to ignore it.

'Kyle helps coach the Amazons,' says Clive.

'The Big K is good for recruitment,' Kyle tells me. 'When the little girls hear that The Kylester's taking training there's always a full attendance. I'm like a movie star to the little girls – a role model – and I take my responsibilities seriously. I like to give a little back to the game that has given me so much.'

I want to be sick but Kyle would probably think that I'm being sick because I'm so impressed with meeting him that I'm overcome with nerves.

'Well, go on with the search, Sherlock. Don't let me stop you.'

If I was on my own I'd admit defeat at this point, go back to my shed, sit down and have a packet of crisps and a Coke and think about Phoebe. But I can't do that with Clive and Kyle watching – they might tell Phoebe

I wasn't working very hard – so I go through the whole room again. I feel really dumb with the two of them watching me, Clive describing everything I do and Kyle describing his greatest goals. All the search gets me is another lungful of dust and a tear in my mother's fleecy mittens from the broken glass. But no clue.

'Sharp's approach seems decidedly unsuccessful,' Clive summarizes.

I decide to try and bluff it out. I can just see Kyle running off to Phoebe and telling her that I'm getting nowhere. She might decide to take me off the case. She looked like someone who'd shout at you if you were doing things right so what would she be like if you got things wrong?

'Right,' I say to Clive, trying to sound confident. 'I think I've got everything I need from here. I'll be off now. Thanks for coming down to open the place up.'

'Sharp leaves the clubhouse to the boos and jeers of the crowd having achieved nothing for his side,' says Clive.

'Yes, I have,' I tell him.

'The expensive new signing for the Amazon side turns out to be a failure, eh Freakshow?' adds Kyle.

'Look,' I say. 'Just because you haven't spotted what I've discovered doesn't mean anything. I'm a skilled detective. I don't give away what I've found out to someone who is a suspect themselves.'

41

'Me?' Kyle says. 'Why am I a suspect?'

'I suspect everyone,' I say.

I heard someone say it on the TV once. It sounded good then. It sounds stupid now.

'Even your mum?' says Clive unhelpfully.

'We don't need to talk about my mum,' I tell him.

'He suspects everyone, Freakshow,' says Kyle and he starts laughing. 'Everyone. Shame he's only got three days to eliminate the world from his enquiries. The Kylester is not impressed.'

I don't like this moron laughing at me.

'Sadly,' he carries on, 'The Big K can't stick around to teach you how to be a detective. There are lots of lonely girls out there and only one Kylester. My time is precious and my hair needs a mirror.'

He walks over and tries to pat me on the side of the cheek with his hand. I pull my head back. However tough he is I'm not just going to let him humiliate me. His hand flashes past my face. It's not very clean considering he's just been in the shower. He'd never get to sit down for tea at my house without my father going mad.

'See you, Sherlock.'

And with that he gives me one last smirk and swaggers off back to the dressing room. I'm not exactly sorry to see him go. But it's no fun to hear him laughing as he does. I wish Clive would go with him but I think he's staying. He's not only staying, he's still talking.

'And the detective has still failed to ask the most obvious question,' he says. 'And he hasn't found the most obvious clue.'

'Like you'd know,' I say.

'Yes, I would,' says Clive. 'The most obvious question is how did the thief get into the clubhouse without breaking open the door?'

It's difficult to admit but he has a point there. So, I decide not to admit it and try and look like I'd thought of it already.

'And the most obvious clue,' he continues and he stands away from the door, 'is here.'

'A doorway?' I say.

'Look closer, Mr Big Shot,' he says.

I walk over to the doorway. I look at it. I don't see anything but a doorway and they don't steal trophies.

'Warmer,' says Clive.

I look up. Nothing. I look down. Sticking out of the door frame about level with my waist is a nail. And hanging on that nail is a bit of pink. I pull it off and drop it on the floor because it's difficult to grip anything properly in mittens. I'm fed up with them anyway so I take them off and pick up the pink thing from the floor.

'What does that tell you?' says Clive.

'Nothing,' I tell him. 'What does it tell you?'

'What's the material?'

I feel the material. It feels slippy.

'I don't know.'

'It's from a football shirt.'

'So,' I say. 'It's from a football shirt. What a big surprise. This is a football club and someone's been wearing a football top. What are you going to prove to me next? That people take exercise books to school or that children's TV presenters haven't got brains? Something really shocking like that?'

He doesn't look any less confident so I figure he must have something else up his sleeve.

'There's only one team around here that play in pink,' he tells me and I know what he's going to say next, 'and that's ...' He pauses dramatically so I finish his sentence off for him.

'The Blondel Babes.'

'Finally, when presented with an open goal, the detective manages to score.'

I think of something nasty to say to him. The thing is he seems to have a point. He's doing much better detective work than me.

'And so all you need to do is find which member of the Blondel Babes has got a hole in her shirt and you know who took the trophy. Even you ought to be able to work it out from there.'

'Thanks,' I say sarcastically. I put the piece of pink shirt in my pocket and head for the door. I don't need to see Clive's smug smile one second longer than I have to.

I get out. The last half hour has been no fun. Being humiliated by idiots is never a good way to spend time. I give a can a good kick as I head over towards my bike. It flies through the air and bounces off my handlebars. I don't know why but I always kick cans when I've got a problem even though it's not going to solve them. It's not a good idea this time though. It's a paint can not a drink can and it smashes into my bike and leaves a grey stain on the frame. Just one more problem to add to Walton's detention and the mystery of the pink piece of football top. I head back to the shed. I need a coke.

CHAPTER 6

Next day, I'm no further on. I've got no definite knowledge about who stole the trophy and I've managed to get myself a detention with Walton. My only lead is one small bit of pink football shirt. I'm not exactly feeling confident. I figure that the thing I've got to do next is find out more about the Blondel Babes and then I'm going to have to get access to their football tops. That sounds rather rude but I know what I mean. If you've got a trail you've got to follow it.

'*Mickey, où est la voiture?*'

'What?'

I look up at Miss Hardy who is staring at me. Unfortunately I shouldn't be doing all my thinking in a French lesson.

'*Où est la voiture?*'

'Pardon, miss,' I smile at Miss Hardy. She's not too bad really. It's just that she keeps trying to make me speak French.

'*Regarde!*' she says and then because I don't understand she waves a worksheet at me. I look down. There's one on my desk. I look at it. I don't understand a word of it. I look up again and shake my head. Her face starts to go a little red which happens when she's angry. Sometimes, after teaching our class, she looks like a ripe tomato.

'*Mon Dieu, Mickey. Où est la voiture?*'

You've got to feel sorry for Miss Hardy. She thinks French is wonderful and she's very good at it and she spends her whole life trying to teach people like me about it. It's no wonder she goes mad sometimes. I decide to have a go to make her feel better.

'*La voiture est …*' I start. Then I can't remember the next bit. '*La voiture est …*' So I say it again.

'*Oui,*' she says, so I must be on the right lines. Maybe if I say it a third time she'll help me out. '*La voiture est …*' I stop and look at her trying to give her the impression that I know the next word, I really know it and it's on the tip of my tongue and that normally I'd just say it right away but, for some strange reason, it's just disappeared from my brain.

'*Dans,*' she says. It works.

'*La voiture est dans …*' I say and then I look at her for help again. Normally if you delay a teacher long enough they'll tell you the answer and then you'll repeat it and you can both pretend that you've learnt something.

Instead she folds her arms and closes her mouth firmly. I've had all the help I'm going to get. I start again.

'*La voiture est dans le …*' I begin. She keeps staring. '*Le …*' She starts getting redder. '*Le … le … le aujourd' hui.*'

'*Non.*' She shakes her head.

'*Le pantalons?*'

'*Non.*'

'*Le soleil brille?*'

'*Non, non, non.*'

'*Eurotunnel?*'

'*Sacrè bleu.*'

'*Disney World Paris?*'

'Mickey. *Sors!*'

'What?'

'*Sors immediatement!*'

'What?'

'Get out of my classroom. I've been teaching you French for three years and you can't even say that the car is in the garage. Do you know what the French is for garage? It's *garage*. It's not very hard, is it? Now get out and stop wasting my time.'

So, I get out. The cheers of the morons at the back are finally cut off when I close the door behind me.

The corridor's empty. I lean against the wall. It's funny when you're in the corridor on your own. Normally it's full of kids pushing each other and

48

teachers telling them not to push each other and kids ignoring the teachers and pushing each other again and the teachers shouting and the kids still pushing and this happening time and time again. Walton goes on at assembly about how this is all terrible and how we all ought to be able to walk down the corridor like civilized people rather than like a football crowd and how one day someone will get seriously injured and then it will be TOO LATE to learn from our mistakes. I reckon it's not the kids' fault. I figure it's the school's fault because school turns kids into robots. Every time a bell goes we have to pick up all our stuff and go somewhere else. It's like we're programmed to respond to a bell. And this goes on every day of every week of every month of every year. So, what happens? You get a whole load of kids who don't think but just plod round the school like robots every time a bell goes. And what happens when a whole load of robots going one way bang into a whole load of robots going the other way? They all just keep walking into each other and it's a complete mess. And then Walton blames the kids. That's rubbish. You don't see kids walking into each other all the time anywhere else and that's because outside school they're not robots.

Anyway, at the moment the corridor's empty and you could almost kid yourself that school is a nice quiet place – if you can ignore the odd scream from the nearest classrooms.

I take a look at the pictures on the wall. Because it's the French corridor, everything is about French, so on one board there's a display about French cheeses and on another there's a picture of a house with all the different parts labelled with their French words. Except that someone's written over them all and so the bit that points to the windows says 'le buttocks' and the bit pointing to the door says 'le breasts' and the bit pointing to the garage says 'le testicles'. It was a good thing I didn't say that to Miss Hardy.

And then, as my eyes flick down the display boards, I see it. Another poster advertising the Blondel Babes. I get over to it fast and rip it straight off the wall. I don't want Walton reappearing and doing another of his helpful tearing-up exercises.

This time I get to read to the bottom of the page. IF INTERESTED, CONTACT: KATIE PIERCE 9B

Katie Pierce. I'm so shocked I stop breathing for about five seconds. Then I realize that it's a stupid thing to do so I start again. Katie Pierce is this girl in our form. She's a complete pain. Her mother's a school governor so all the teachers let her get away with everything. She never does any work and is always chatting but she never gets into trouble. And even when she does her mother just comes into school and before you know it she's out of trouble again. She gets put into top set for everything even though she's lazy and she thinks she's God's gift to boys. She is really good looking but she's a one-girl lesson in the fact that looks aren't all that matter. All the boys who have ever gone out with her get turned into her little servants and after a while you see them hanging around behind her looking miserable and frightened and desperate to emigrate. The lucky ones she finishes with quickly, the unlucky ones are told that it's 'serious'. They end up in these relationships which can last up to six weeks. One of her boyfriends spent two weeks hiding from her in the boys' toilets every breaktime. She went in and dragged him out in the end and then finished with him in front of the whole playground. His family moved to Wales three weeks later.

And she hates me. It's long and complicated but basically, after a whole load of provocation, I got her caught smoking. She got into trouble and she's sworn to get me back.

And that's the strange thing. What was Katie Pierce who spends every breaktime and lunchtime smoking and who drives our PE teacher mad by faking injuries at the start of every PE lesson (she got out of PE last week by saying that she pulled a muscle in her arm putting on her make-up), what was she doing getting involved with an under-12 girls' football team? If this girl broke a nail during a game of hockey she'd threaten to sue the school for inflicting post-traumatic stress. This girls hates sports. So, what was she doing with the Blondel Babes?

There was nothing for it. I was going to have to ask her.

CHAPTER 7

It's not difficult to find Katie Pierce at lunchtime – you just look for the biggest plumes of smoke. Her and her gang never stop smoking. Mind you, loads of people at our school smoke. The guy who owns the newsagents' across the road has got a brand new BMW. I don't get the smoking thing at all. I mean I've tried once or twice. I used to think that, if so many people spent so much money then there must be something good about it, whatever they said on the TV, so I bought ten and smoked a couple. They make you cough, feel sick and your mouth tastes disgusting for about ten hours afterwards. And they give you cancer if you smoke them for long enough. People are mad. They pay to be poisoned.

Still, I decide that Katie Pierce's group are not going to be the most receptive audience for a discussion on fags. Smoking is the only thing some of them can do well. Katie's the queen of her gang. She's one of these people who can't be in anything if anyone ever gets more attention than her. She hates it if anybody is prettier or cleverer.

Her gang stand around her. There's her best friend Julie Reece. She's better looking than Katie but she has to pretend she's not. Katie gets really jealous if Julie gets more attention from boys and says horrible stuff to Julie really loudly about her dad running off with his secretary. Julie goes mad if boys ever ask her out when Katie's around because then she gets picked on even more. I don't understand girls. They have best friends and they spend the whole time arguing with each other and 'dissing' each other and writing nasty notes about each other to pass around the class. It's more like having best enemies. All boys do with their best friends is play football and have farting competitions.

The rest of the girls in Katie's gang have probably got names and if you looked hard enough they might even have personalities too, though I have my doubts. Basically they just hang around Katie doing bad imitations of her. If Katie gets her hair cut, they'll all get theirs cut the next week. If Katie starts wearing a colour they all start wearing stuff that colour. I reckon if you told them that Katie had gone mad and decided that she was a dog they'd all turn up the next day at school wearing leads.

I wander over to them trying to look like it's a casual visit and I was just passing. I can't see it convincing anybody. Katie Pierce hates me and I know she hates me so why would I wander over for a chat? But I don't want her to know that I'm on a case so that means acting as casually as possible so I don't put her on her guard. It means I'm going to have to try some small talk before I pop my serious questions. It's not going to be easy. I nod as I get near them. None of them nods back. I try and kick my brain for something, anything that is going to make these girls talk to me. How can you follow a trail if the trail stops? You can't unless you're an ancient Red Indian tracker and I'm not. What will make these girls talk to me? Money? I don't have any. Charm? None of that either. I'm stuck, unless …

'Have you heard about the new lad in Year Eleven? He's just got a part in a Levi's commercial and joined a boy band.'

'Who?' says Katie Pierce.

'I've not seen him,' says Julie Reece.

'What's the band's name?' says another girl.

'How do you know?' says another.

'Is he fit?' they all say together.

Got them. What always gets girls your own age interested? Good-looking older boys. Normally it's a pain that all they care about is sixteen-year-olds but this time it's working to my advantage. I mean, it doesn't make sense. Women live longer than men according to our Geography teacher and she's living

55

proof. She might actually be a fossil. So, if women live longer than men then they should be interested in boys younger than them so they don't get left alone in their old age. I figure that I might use this argument on Phoebe one day.

'He's my cousin,' I say. I'm lying. 'I could introduce you.'

They all start looking a bit more friendly. Apart from Katie.

'When, Mickey?' she says. 'I find it hard to believe that someone in your family could be anything other than repulsive.'

She's a lovely girl.

'Well,' I say. 'Seeing is believing. How about … say … 4.30 after school at the Xanadu?' That's a café in town.

They all start making these 'yeah' noises. All except Katie. 'We can't,' she says.

They all look at her.

'Why not?' I say. 'He's just broken up with his girlfriend.'

Their tongues start almost hanging out when I say that.

'Because, Mickey,' she says, 'we are girls of the world. We do not go running after some boy even if he is going to be a model and a pop star. Do we, girls?'

Her friends don't look too convinced when she says

that. They look like they'd break the world hundred-metres record just to *see* a boy who was going to be a model and a pop star, never mind talk to him.

'No, we don't,' they say dutifully. Well, that's what their mouths say. Their eyes say, 'Yes, we do. Yes, we do. Yes, we do.'

'Oh, well,' I say. 'I suppose I'll have to introduce him to somebody else. You see he really wants to get to know some kids at school. He says he doesn't want to be isolated from real people when the pop star thing kicks in and he ends up living permanently in a land of parties and premières with nothing but celebrities and fans. He needs a good woman to be with him during all his success to keep his feet on the ground.'

'Rubbish,' says Katie. She's right. It is. But that's the trouble. Once you've invented a cousin who's about to be a pop star and a model you've got to keep faith with him. The secret to being a good liar is never backing down. It's like when a teacher is telling you off for breaking a window or something and they try to cut a deal with you by saying something like, 'I'm sure you didn't mean to break the window, did you? And I can understand that you're worried about what will happen to you but if you tell me you broke it then it will be much easier to make sure you don't get into any real trouble.' Never go for it.

'You won't know unless you come,' I tell Katie.

'OK, if it's rubbish you can diss me all you like. But you won't know.'

'He's right,' says Julie Reece.

'Yeah,' say the others.

Katie's face goes red when the others agree with me.

'What do you mean, he's right? Are you taking his side against mine? Are you putting him before me?'

One of the great things about girls is that they're never going to make an argument smaller if they can make it bigger. Girls really like big shouting rows with their mates. You see it from a distance and you think that one of them's just murdered the other's pet hamster and eaten it for their tea and then you get up close and it turns out that one of them didn't notice that the other one had got a new top on.

There's a pause while the others decide whether to stand up to Katie. The betting is about 100–1 against.

'We could just check it out,' says Julie. Somebody just won a hundred pounds. 'I mean, if he's there, then you know a pop star and a model and if he's not then we can diss this weedy piece of nothing.'

I decide the time is not quite right to take issue with the 'weedy piece of nothing' line.

'Yeah,' say the other girls.

'We can't,' says Katie.

'Yeah we can,' says Julie.

'No, we can't.'

'Yes, we can.'

'No, we can't.'

This is like the pantomimes that my old Uncle Brendan used to take us to when we were little. He used to get drunk and shout out, 'Whatever happened to compromise?' and then start laughing at what he'd said. I never got the joke. Me and my sister used to try and pretend we weren't with him. My sister was so good at pretending she wasn't with him that one year she tried to go home with another family.

'Why not?' I interrupt. You have to stop this "Yes I can/No you can't" stuff with girls straight away. Otherwise it can go on for hours. At least with boys it will lead to something quickly. Usually violence.

'Yeah, why not?' say the others.

'Because ...' says Katie.

'Yeah?' they all say.

'Because ...' Her face goes red.

'Yeah?'

'Because I've got football training.'

There's a pause.

'What?' they all shriek. My ears start ringing. It's as though they've found out that she's going out with a Year Seven boy with spots and bad breath.

'Football,' says Julie. 'But that's, like, exercise.'

'Uncool,' say all the others.

Katie goes red when they say that. I don't think that anyone in her gang has ever dared call her 'uncool' before.

'It's his fault,' she almost spits at me when she says it.

'Me?' I say. Well actually, I squeak. My voice is a bit unreliable at the moment. All of a sudden I'll open my mouth to speak and a noise will come out that only dogs can hear. It's because my voice is breaking and getting deeper according to those silly books they give us in Personal and Social Education, the ones which seem to be mostly about hair growing everywhere. Although why a voice, if it wants to get deeper, can't just get deeper instead of taking a detour through all the highest notes it can think of is beyond me.

'You,' says Katie. I'm surprised. I never realized I had so much power.

'He sent those photos to my mum that showed me smoking and she said that I had to get involved in something that was "beneficial to the community" in order to make up for having "a foul personal habit" and she knows one of the women involved in this stupid under-12 girls' football team and they didn't have a manager so now I have to be it. And my mother does random breath tests on me. She'll suddenly grab my head and start sniffing my breath to see if there's any trace of fags. I'm spending more on mints these days than I am on cigarettes. It's a nightmare.'

So, now I know. After all that trouble and lying I find out that Katie Pierce is involved with the girls' football team because of me. That doesn't explain why she'd want to nick a trophy. If she's *got* to do it she wouldn't care whether they win or lose.

'You talk to girls in Year Seven?' says Julie Reece.

'Loser,' say her friends.

'I'm going to stop,' says Katie desperately. 'My mum says I can stop if the team win the cup final this weekend. That will show I've achieved something good to make up for doing something bad.'

'What if you lose?' says Julie.

'I've got to do another year,' says Katie. 'But I won't lose.'

'How do you know?' I say.

'Believe me, Mickey,' Katie says, 'there are some things that a girl just knows.'

Now things are beginning to fall into place. She's got to win and if I know Katie when it's her coolness at stake she won't be bothered about obeying any rules. She must have got the trophy. But I can't just accuse her. That would give her a warning. She'd never admit it. So, now I've got to try and work out what she's done with it. I figure that turning up at training might be the best place to start. Well, actually, it's the only place to start. But at least I'm getting somewhere and …

'Mickey.'

My brain stops whizzing round. Julie Reece is talking to me.

'We'll be at the Xanadu at 4.30. He'd better be worth it.'

The other girls nod. I don't know what they're nodding for. Then, it clicks back into my mind. My cousin. Pop star and model. This is what improvising does for you. Just when you're happy to give up on a lie someone else starts believing it. I can't tell them that he doesn't exist or else Katie might start wondering what I was really interested in.

So, I nod.

They head off towards the school, practising their sexy walks all the way.

Where am I going to find a potential model and pop star in need of friends and get him in the Xanadu by 4.30? The only people I know are ugly and can't sing. Now, if they were good-looking and couldn't sing we'd be getting somewhere. I need help.

CHAPTER 8

'Move. The 15.32 is due in at platform three and your hand is blocking its entry to the station. I don't want a repeat of the fiasco which occurred when my mother brought my tea up here and spilt ketchup all over the 17.23.'

I move my hand. The train chugs by and arrives safely in the station. David blows his whistle.

'The 15.32 just arrived at platform three was two minutes late due to a hand on the line. We apologize to our customers for any inconvenience caused by the delay and hope that we will be seeing them soon in the future.'

David is never going to be a model. He's never going to be a pop star. But he's my only hope because none of the girls will ever have seen him before. They won't have seen him because he spends his whole life stuck in his attic playing with his huge model railway which hasn't given him the best complexion in the world. But if he can go to the Xanadu for fifteen minutes and say he's going to be a pop star and a model, then who'll know? I've got his story all worked out. He can tell them that he's going to be a model for a new acne product – the one who hasn't used the product yet – and he can say he makes dance music on his computer. They're always so ugly the guys who make dance records. It's just that they always wear baseball caps so you can't see. I've nicked a baseball cap out of my sister's bedroom. If only he'd give it a chance.

'You've put my timetable behind,' he tells me.

I apologize.

'My reputation depends on the accurate arrival times of my trains.'

I apologize again. He shakes his head.

'Fancy doing me a favour?' I ask. It's not the best time to ask but I've got no choice.

'Anything to do with trains?' David asks. He starts rubbing his glasses clean. They got all steamed up when the train was late.

'Not exactly,' I tell him. 'It's more to do with girls.'

'Eeeuu,' he says. It's a noise and it's not a positive one.

'What?' I say.

'I don't have anything to do with girls,' he says, 'after the incident with the signal box.'

'The signal box?' I ask. The idea of David and a girl in a signal box sounds interesting.

'I don't talk about it.' His whole body shakes at the memory.

'Oh,' I say.

'But my points were damaged irreparably.'

I try to look shaken.

'And it was at the weekend,' he says. 'A bank-holiday weekend. My network was shut down for days. I was only operating a skeleton service at the time but …'

'David. Shut up.'

He's in danger of getting hysterical. I look at my watch. It's five to four. It will take him half an hour to get to the Xanadu. I've got five minutes to convince him to pretend to be a model and pop star. I have the feeling that he's not going to go voluntarily.

I pick up the nearest train.

'Put that down,' he barks.

I throw it in the air.

He gasps.

I catch it.

He starts breathing heavily.

'Put that down,' he says again. 'That's a limited edition model of The Flying Scotsman.'

'David,' I tell him. 'I need a favour. You have to do me the favour. I'd like to persuade you but I haven't got the time. If you don't agree I'm going to find out if The Flying Scotsman can really fly.'

'You wouldn't,' he says.

'I would,' I tell him. It's an obvious line but you've got to say it in these situations.

He stares at me. I stare back. I can see his mind battling, weighing up his love for The Flying Scotsman against his hatred of girls.

The Flying Scotsman wins.

'All right,' he says.

In five minutes I've got him standing outside, out of his guard's uniform, dressed in some clothes that make him look at least a bit human and up-to-date with what he's got to do. And all that time I keep a tight hold on The Flying Scotsman.

'I'll get you back for this,' he says.

I chuck him a couple of pounds.

'Have a Pleasure Dome on me,' I tell him. They are these really big cakes they do in the Xanadu.

He pockets the money.

'I'll give you your train back later.'

'If you hurt one piston on her engine,' he tells me, 'I'll find you and be revenged. I have friends at the Train-spotters' Club who can do very nasty things with a guard's flag.'

I try not to look too scared.

'Get moving,' I tell him. 'My reputation depends on accurate arrival times.'

He walks off. I jump on my bike and head off in the other direction. I don't want to be late for the Blondel Babes' training session.

CHAPTER 9

I have to pedal like anything to get there on time. I don't really know what I expect to find but you've got to follow the trail. Then maybe you'll stumble on something.

The Blondel Babes' ground is part of a park. There's some swings and a roundabout and some flowers and stuff. As parks go around where I live it's not too bad. Some of the swings haven't been vandalized and there's not that much broken glass. The Babes' ground is a bit nicer than the one that the Amazons have got. The white lines aren't quite as wavy and the nets haven't got massive holes in them.

Already there are about twenty girls on the pitch running around and doing those bending and stretching exercises which are supposed to make sure you don't get injured. I look for some cover. I don't want Katie Pierce to know I'm there, so I need to check the team out from a distance. There's a couple of bushes and a tree nearby so I head for them. The bushes are actually pretty big and thick, which is good news as there's no chance that anybody will see me. I push my way in and then I stop. There's a kind of little hollow bit in the middle of these bushes and in it are two people. A boy and a girl. They are lying on the ground and they are kissing. They've both got their eyes closed.

'Really fancy you,' says the boy and kisses her some more.

'Really?' says the girl.

'Really, really fancy you,' says the boy.

'Really, really?' says the girl.

And then she opens her eyes. And screams.

I realize that I'm not in the best position to explain myself so I try to put on a friendly smile.

'Pervert,' the girl yells.

It doesn't help that I've got my dad's binoculars in my hand.

She stands up, pushes past me and battles her way out of the bushes. You can hear the stream of swear words gradually disappearing into the distance.

The boy looks at me.

'Sorry,' I offer.

He shakes his head. 'Sorry ain't going to get you out of this one.'

'Very sorry,' I try.

It doesn't have any visible effect. A bit like when

a teacher yells at our class to shut up last lesson on a Friday.

'Girls, eh?' I shrug. 'Can't live with them, Can't live … Ow!'

After a while my nose stops hurting and I turn my attention to the training session. There's a gap in the bush for me to poke my binoculars through so I get a pretty good view. They're playing football now. They're like any group of eleven-year-olds playing football. They all run round after the ball. As soon as they get it they try to dribble past everybody else. They never pass and they all shout at each other. I recognize one of the kids. Little Justine Bird from my primary school. You don't normally remember little kids from primary school but I'll always remember Justine Bird. That's because we once had this assembly on the things to do if a stranger asks you to get into his car. Justine Bird had to do this speech and you could tell she was really nervous. Her face was all red and she kept swaying from side to side like one of those cheap fat round toys that mean relations give you for Christmas. And then in the middle of the speech this little puddle started appearing by her feet and it kept growing and you could tell she knew it was happening but she didn't stop or run away. It was like she couldn't move. And nobody laughed because it was just too horrible to laugh at. And it seemed to go on for hours but it was probably only ten seconds. And then some teacher spotted it and took her away. And then the headteacher carried on with the assembly all the time pretending that she wasn't standing by a big pool of wee. That's the only assembly I've ever remembered for more than five minutes and that's because it went wrong. Assemblies that go right are more boring than an evening playing cards with my grandmother.

I spot Katie. She's sitting on a chair with her legs crossed, not even watching the football. In fact, she's filing her nails. And smoking. And chewing. My dad's binoculars are very good. He bought them in the days before he lost his job when everything new in our house didn't have to be the cheapest thing in the shop. All the coaching seems to be being done by this person in a black tracksuit. I focus the binoculars on him for ages trying to see if I know him but I can't get a good enough look. He's got one of those tracksuits with a hood on and he keeps it up and drawn really tight. He must be sweating a bit because it's still pretty hot. Still some people will do anything to look cool. It's like those rappers you see on *Top of the Pops*. It must be boiling in the studio with all the lights and screaming girls and them dancing but they've still got these big thick puffa jackets on. I don't get rap. Why do people want to listen to other people shouting at them about how good they are and how rubbish everybody else is? If they want that, they can just go to an assembly with our headteacher.

So, I watch the football training. I've never really watched girls play football before. I mean sometimes you see one try and join in with the boys at lunchtime but the boys don't let them. They say that girls aren't any good at football and spoil it. It's not really that surprising that they aren't as good as boys if nobody ever lets them play. I don't reckon that boys stop girls playing football because they aren't any good but because they're frightened that they might turn out to be better than them. Because if a girl starts beating a boy at football then the boy loses face with all his mates. So, as soon as a girl starts trying to play football boys start messing around and making it really obvious to everybody that they're not trying because then if she dribbles past them or even scores a goal they can pretend that it only happened because they weren't taking the game seriously. Boys like it much better when girls stand on the touchline admiring them. They think that's what a girl's job is. I think girls are right to start playing football though. If you had to stand and watch some of the head cases who play for our school teams and pretend to admire them, you'd get bored pretty soon too.

There's an extra loud blast on the whistle. The

girls all come together in a circle. Mr Trying-To-Be-Cool-In-The-Black-Tracksuit stands in the middle and starts coaching them, telling them about how a thing called passing might be a good idea. I mean I know I think that girls should play football but this lot weren't. They were just playing running after the ball and screaming. I'd guess they've got no chance of beating the Amazons and I've never even seen the Amazons play. The Blondel Babes would struggle to beat a group of toddlers as far as I can see. How they ever got to the final is a complete mystery.

'What's all this then?'

I jump and bite my tongue at the same time. This hurts.

'Eeeh,' I splutter.

'Don't try and act foreign with me, lad. I know all the tricks. I've been at this game man and boy for forty-five years and I've seen it all, from sick on the roundabout to bubble bath in the fountain. Don't try any nonsense with me.'

The old man who says this is wearing a green uniform with a badge on which it says J. COBB, PARK ATTENDANT. He's holding some kind of thing my dad used to use when he was gardening (before he got all depressed and stopped). I think it's called a hoe. Anyway, whatever it's called, at the moment it looks like it's going to be used as a weapon.

'Now, there's been reports of a young girl leaving these here bushes screaming. What do you know about that?'

'Nothing,' I say, giving him my best innocent look.

'Don't come the old "nothing" game with me, sonny. I've been in this game too long for people to be saying "nothing" to me. I knows when a boy's up to mischief. Now out with it.'

He grips the hoe tighter and lifts it up a bit.

I tell him again that I don't know anything. His eyes lock on to my binoculars.

'What are you doing with them, then?'

This is a bit more difficult. I don't really fancy telling the old guy that what I was doing was spying on some eleven-year-old girls doing football training – it would make me sound like a right weirdo. On the other hand, having stonewalled over the girl in the bushes, I don't want to annoy him too much by not coming up with some explanation for the binoculars – he might decide to call the police which is just what I don't need at the moment.

'Come on, lad,' he says, 'don't think you can make me go away just by giving me the silent treatment. I've been in this park forty-five years so a five-minute wait isn't going to make me get bored and go away. I'll stand here until there's weeds in every border in the Jubilee Gardens if necessary, so think on. I'm not a man who lacks patience.'

Have you noticed that the older adults get the happier they are with just saying the same things all the time? It's like my grandmother. Every time she comes round she tells me to think about the sacrifices Jesus made for me and clean my teeth more regularly. I figure that as you get older and your life gets more boring you run out of new things to say because your brain slows down and so you just keep saying the same stuff over and over again. And then when you get really old you forget most of the things that you used to say all the time. So, you're left with about three things to say and you say them non-stop. All old people do it.

'I'm still here, lad,' the keeper reminds me.

I need to think of some kind of explanation for the binoculars, quick. Some kind of innocent hobby that requires hiding in bushes. There is one. I know there's one. I can feel it coming to me.

'Molewatching,' I say proudly.

As soon as it's out of my mouth I knew it should have been birdwatching but I was under pressure.

'Molewatching,' the park keeper repeats.

I nod. I've got to stick to it now.

'Moles, lad, live underground.'

I nod again.

'You can't see them from above ground, lad.'

This could be a problem.

'I know,' I say. 'That's what makes the hobby so challenging. I used to be a bird-watcher but it was too easy. You just look up in the sky and there they are. Where's the fun in that?'

I can see that I've got him puzzled. His face crinkles up like a crisp with ridges.

'But …' he says. And then he stops. He knows there's a 'but' but he can't quite work out what it is. Let's face it, he's a park keeper not a brain surgeon.

'Can I carry on now?' I say. 'I had my binoculars on a piece of earth and I spotted a tremor. There could be a hill beginning.'

He stares at me as though I'm mad. This is a good thing. If people think you're mad they never make you do anything. Well, except go on talk shows in America.

'All right,' he says. 'But let me make one thing clear, lad. It's fine for the likes of you young lads to come down here molewatching but for the likes of us park keepers moles is a menace. The damage they've done to our bowling green. I'd rather have a coachload of drunken football supporters than a mole. They're hooligans. So, next time you see a cute little nose pointing out of the earth, think on.'

I agree to think on. Whatever that means.

'And,' he continues, 'I don't want no more reports of screaming girls coming out of these here bushes or I'll be back. And I won't be carrying a hoe next time. No. I'll be carrying a fork.'

I try to look suitably terrified. He pushes his way out of the bushes.

There's a loud blast on a football whistle. I train my binoculars onto the girls. They go into one final circle with their coach and then start walking off to the changing rooms, a little line of pink.

This is annoying. I was hoping that I'd be able to spot the girl with the piece missing from her football top and now it looks like the chance has gone.

I sit in the bushes trying to work out how to get a minute alone with eleven football strips. No ideas hit me straightaway. A guy walks past the bushes with his dog. The dog stops and squats down to do its business. The guy walks on a bit and pretends he hasn't noticed. Then, when he's got far enough to try and con people that the dog has got nothing to do with him, he stops. All people with dogs are like that. You see them walking down our street sometimes. The dog decides it's got to go and the owner finds out that there's something really interesting he wants to look at on the other side of the road. There's one guy who takes his dog for a walk near us and they always stop right outside our house. I reckon that he must have something against us. It's amazing what adults get away with when you think about it. Imagine if a group of kids started leaving bits of poo outside everybody's houses. That's way more disgusting than dropping a crisp wrapper if you ask me, but because it's kids who drop crisp wrappers everybody has a go at us. Just because it's adults who leave their dogs' business everywhere nothing happens. But which would you prefer to step on by mistake? I'd take the crisp packet every time.

The girls start coming out of the changing room. They come in ones and twos. Some parents are standing outside waiting for them and they go off towards the car park to go home. They've obviously got better dads than mine. You never saw someone happier to get his son a bike. I thought it was because he was being kind at first. Then I realized that it was just because there were even fewer places he had to give me a lift to. They always give my sister lifts to places. They say it's because she's a young girl and they've got to look out for her safety. But because I'm a boy they reckon that I can be risked. Girls get all the best things in this world, whatever Ms Walter says in P.S.E.

After a while the dribble of girls coming out of the changing room stops. I really need to get a look at their shirts. I walk slowly towards the dressing room hut. There's no cover so I just try and look innocent.

I'll be safe as long as Katie Pierce doesn't see me. I glance inside the hut. I can't see anybody. I inch my way in. If anybody stops me I'm going to say I thought it was the toilet. But there's nobody. There's a couple of doors. I open the first one and peer round. It's a changing room all right, but it's empty. Well, there's one old sock on the floor but that's about it. There's always one old sock on the floor of every changing room. Never two, always one.

I try the next door. It's the other changing room and sitting in the middle of the floor is a bag and inside the bag are a heap of pink football shirts.

I flick a quick glance behind me and from side to side. There's nobody around. I move fast. I slip through the door and close it behind me. I'd like to lock it but there isn't a lock. I start dragging the tops out of the bag. Number five is complete. So's number seven. And number three. And number two. And number eleven. And number ... no, wait a minute. There's a tear in number nine. I drag the piece of pink cloth from my pocket. I lay the shirt out flat on the floor. I put the piece of cloth into the hole in the pink shirt. It fits like the final piece of a jigsaw. So, number nine, the centre forward for the Blondel Babes, was at the scene of the crime. I've followed the trail and it has led me to the thief. All I have to do now is find out who plays number nine for the Blondel Babes and face her with the evidence. She's an eleven-year-old girl. She's bound to crack if I act tough. And once she's confessed then the whole scam will fall apart and the Amazons will get the chance to defend their …

'I knew it.'

I swing around. In one hand I've got a piece of pink cloth. In the other hand I've got a pink football shirt with a hole in it.

'I've been doing this job for more years than I can remember and I can spot a young lad up to no good as easy as I can spot a teenager going down the toddlers' slide. Now you just stay where you are.'

It's the park keeper and he's not holding a hoe any more. He's holding a fork. A large fork. And he's pointing it at me.

'I knew you was a bad 'un. I says to myself you keep an eye on that lad an' I kept an eye on you and you didn't see me because I been working in this park more years than you've had hot dinners and I know where to go to keep myself out of sight. Now you just stay where you are.'

I'm not going anywhere. He's standing in front of the only exit and he's got a weapon.

'I suppose you'll want to know what I'm doing here,' I say, trying to sound as mature as possible.

'I don't want no more of your fibs,' he says. 'You just keep quiet.'

He reaches into his pocket and pulls out a mobile phone. He flicks it open and punches in a number. It's a very short number.

Behind him the door opens and Katie Pierce walks in.

'Police, please,' says the park keeper to the phone.

'Hey,' I shout. 'You don't need to do that. Look, this is Katie, she'll tell you that I'm not doing anything wrong.'

He turns round and looks at Katie. She smiles sweetly at the park keeper.

'I've never seen this boy before in my life,' she tells him.

CHAPTER 10

'I have never been so embarrassed in my life.'

'What's wrong with you, Mickey?'

'Is that why we brought you up, sacrificed so much, so that we could be hauled down to the police station to find our only son is a criminal?'

'Do you enjoy making us unhappy?'

'You'll come to a bad end.'

'We're going to toughen up the discipline at home, Mickey. We've been too easy with you and you've gone wild.'

My mum and dad take it in turns to abuse me on the way back. They had to come down to the police station to get me. There's some law apparently that till you're sixteen you have to have your parents there when the police interview you. I was accused of attempting to steal a girl's football strip and behaving strangely in the bushes. Well, actually behaving strangely in the bushes isn't a crime so they called it something else but that's what it meant. It sounded terrible the way the policeman said it. The fact that I'd told the park keeper I was molewatching didn't help much. I mean it was a lie but it was hardly the biggest one in the world. The policeman and my parents acted like it was as bad as being a serial killer. The policeman kept saying they'd have to take me down to the cells and I'd be in there all night which I didn't fancy much because they always have drunk people in police cells on the TV and I didn't want anybody being sick on me. The policeman obviously thought I was trying to play some kind of trick on somebody so I told him that I was. Always tell adults what they want to hear – it's much easier than telling them the truth. Then, after a whole load of shouting at me and my mum telling the policeman that I was a good boy really and I always helped round the house, the copper told me that I was very lucky and they were going to give me a chance. My mum said I had to say thank you to the nice policeman so I said thank you, pretending I meant it. But I didn't really. I mean I was trying to solve a crime and who comes along and stops me but a policeman. And I'm supposed to thank him for it.

It's fairly late by the time we get home. My parents have run out of abuse and have started on a combination of hostile silence (my dad) and disappointed sighs (my mum).

'Get to bed,' says my dad as soon as we're through the door. 'We'll decide your punishment in the morning.'

This sounds a bit worrying as it means he's going to have all night to think about it. He might come up with something really nasty if he takes that much time. I say sorry for the millionth time and shoot up the stairs. The last thing I want is to spend any more time with my parents. As I go past the toilet door I hear what sounds like my sister being sick again. She must have some kind of food poisoning. I wait outside the door because I've got to clean my teeth. The toilet flushes and she comes out. I ask her if she's OK.

'What?' she snaps.

'You were being sick again,' I tell her.

'No, I wasn't. Shut up,' she says. Then she shoves past me, thumps down to her room and slams the door behind her. That's what you get for being nice.

I go into the toilet and lock the door behind me. It's the only room in our house with a lock. So, in the one place where I won't get hassled, I sit down to work out what I've discovered. I know that Katie Pierce has a motive for stealing the cup and I know that the number nine of the Blondel Babes was involved in it (or at least her shirt was). To find this out has cost me one detention with Walton, a visit to the police station, the admiration of my parents (which, let's face it, wasn't really there to begin with) and the discovery by the chief suspect that I'm on her case. Things are not exactly going well.

'Mickey is a pervert. Mickey is a pervert.'

What a great way to start the school day. The morons at the back have got a new song.

'Mickey is a pervert. Mickey is a pervert.'

I flick a look at Katie Pierce. She's in for once and she's got a big smug smile on her face. I try to look like I don't care but it's not too convincing. Not only has she rumbled what I'm up to with her football team, she's also managed to humiliate me in front of my entire peer group. I could be traumatized for life if you believe what Ms Walter says in P.S.E. Still, traumatizing people for life is Katie Pierce's idea of fun.

'Sit down and be quiet for the register.' Mr Newman arrives, which at least stops the morons singing their stupid song.

'Sir, did you know there's a pervert in the class?'

'He steals little girls' clothes.'

'He's going to grow up to be a serial killer, sir.'

'We shouldn't be in the same class as him.'

'It's disgusting.'

'Mickey …' says Mr Newman.

The class all cheer when he says my name.

'How did you know it was him, sir?'

'Has he done it before?'

'SHUT UP,' screams Mr Newman. The class shuts up. 'Now I don't know what you're talking about and I don't want to know. Mickey, Mr Walton would like to see you immediately. Something to do with a missed detention. Off you go. Oh, and Mr Walton said you'll need an escort to make sure you don't get inexplicably lost on the way. Katie, would you go with him?'

Trust a teacher to make the worst possible choice in the world.

'I can't, sir,' says Katie.

'What?' says Newman.

'I'd love to do what you ask, but it would be too dangerous. You see, Mickey can't really be trusted with an attractive girl like myself.'

'What?' says Newman, whose mouth is hanging open.

'To be blunt, sir,' says Katie. 'Mickey is a deviant. I doubt he will ever successfully relate to the opposite sex.'

The morons give a sort of cheer when she says that. They don't understand it but they'll cheer any sentence with the word 'sex' in because they think it must be rude. Half the boys in the world are like that.

'What?' says Newman again. I think he might be turning into a moron himself. Teachers do get stupider as they get older. Their brain cells all die. We did it in Biology.

'I'll go,' says Julie Reece.

'What?' says Newman for the fourth time.

'Perverts are just up your street, aren't they?' Katie says to Julie.

'OK,' says Newman. 'I don't care. Julie, you make sure Mickey gets to Mr Walton's office and can everybody stop saying "pervert" and shut up? I've got a headache.'

Now, that is a stupid thing to say. A teacher who tells a class that he's got a headache is just asking for more noise. But I've got to go and see Walton so I don't get a chance to hear it happen.

I find out why Julie volunteered to take me down to Walton as soon as we get outside. 'Mickey,' she says. 'Could you put a word in for me with your cousin? I think he's really cute.'

There are times when the world stops making sense and this is one of those times.

'Uuh?' I say. I'm too shocked to be able to say a proper word.

'Your cousin,' she says. 'He doesn't have a girlfriend, does he?'

'Eeeh?' I reply. I'm still incapable of saying real things.

'So, you know, give him a hint.'

I cannot believe this. If you wanted to design the world's least attractive boy you'd probably invent David. He stares at the floor all the time, dresses like a teacher and hasn't heard of the concept of personal hygiene. 'You fancy him?' I say.

'Don't be so immature,' she says. 'It's deeper than that. He's different from other boys. He's older and more sensitive and he doesn't boast about the great future he's got ahead of him in modelling and pop music.'

She bought it. She really bought it. She really believes he's sixteen and he's going to be famous. If only she knew he was a fourteen-year-old social reject and the biggest future event he could look forward to is a trip to the station, I bet she wouldn't be calling him deep and sensitive and asking me to put in a good word.

'Er … OK,' I tell her.

She smiles.

'So, when will he be on the TV?' she says. 'He's so modest that he wouldn't actually tell us any dates or anything.'

'What did he tell you about his new career?' I say to avoid answering the question.

'Nothing really. He hardly said anything apart from hello, and some stuff about trains. He's so modest, when he could be talking about modelling and being a pop star. He's so deep.'

We get to Walton's office.

'Thanks, Mickey,' she says.

'No problem,' I tell her.

She starts walking back to class.

'Julie,' I call after her.

She turns back round.

'What do you think of trains?'

'Trains?' She looks a bit confused. 'There's nothing to think about trains, is there?'

Pity. It could have been the beginning of a beautiful relationship.

CHAPTER 11

So, Walton gives me the lecture. How badly behaved I am, how rude I am, how much trouble I cause, how I'm going to ruin my education, how I'm going to fail all my exams, how I'm going to leave school and find that the world outside is a cruel and unforgiving place, how I will never amount to anything, how I will watch as my school mates progress into good jobs and successful relationships whilst I am doomed for ever to be a social outcast and how I will end my life bitter and twisted with a massive sense of waste and failure.

It seems a big prediction to make on the grounds of me not showing up for one detention if you ask me.

It's a crazy world when you think about it. Kids who can be bothered to learn the past tense in French and what soil erosion does in the Nile Delta get good lives and the ones who can think of better things to do like working out why all teachers wear such lousy clothes and always look depressed get nothing. No wonder all the people in important jobs are boring – they had their brains destroyed learning about soil erosion.

Anyway, after he's given me the lecture he tells me that he's going to give me two extra detentions and he's going to send a letter home about my behaviour. I'm going to be even more popular than normal at home this weekend. First the police, now the school. Sometimes you get the feeling that everybody is out to get you. And I've got a spot in my ear. Till you've had a spot in your ear you don't know what pain is.

I head back to lessons. It's Drama and by the time I get there they've all got into groups and started improvising a scene about bullying. Drama lessons are always the same. Mr Johns gives us the day's theme and then we all have to get into groups and devise and improvise some scene for half an hour and then we take it in turns to show it to the class. Mr Johns always says that Drama is about conflict and that means that the scenes are always the same – the boys' groups all have fights and the girls' groups call each other bitches. I don't see what it teaches you except maybe how to get a part in *EastEnders*.

Mr Johns isn't too happy about me being late. He strokes his stupid goatee beard and tells me that I'll be poisoning the dynamic or something if I join a group now. So, I've got to go and sit in the corner and prepare a monologue about being bullied. I don't know what a monologue is. He says it's when somebody stands by themselves and says whatever comes into their head. A bit like my gran.

Not being in a group is fine with me. It means that instead of avoiding getting thumped by the morons at the back, who have a big belief that drama should be as realistic as possible, I can think about how I'm going to crack the case. The trouble is I'm stuck. I know who I think stole the trophy but that means nothing. I can't go back to Phoebe with a piece of pink football strip and say here's the solution to your case. She'd go mad and probably say 'period' a hundred times and I'd end up looking like a tomato. It would be stupid to try and accuse Katie Pierce. She'd just laugh in my face and call me a pervert. The only place the trail is leading is to the number-nine shirt of the Blondel Babes and that isn't any use because I don't know who plays centre forward.

But Justine Bird does.

The thought hits me like a thump from one of the morons at the back. I'd remembered Justine Bird from primary school but I'd forgotten that by now she's in Year Seven. I'm so stupid. It's like just because the last time I saw her she was wetting herself in primary school I think she's always going to be in primary school. You forget people get older.

'Mickey.'

I look up. Mr Johns is standing over me.

'You seem to have totally immersed yourself in the task,' he says. 'The class await your monologue with anticipation.'

'It's not quite ready,' I say.

'Nonsense,' he says. 'The rawness of the performance will give it a cutting edge. Come into the centre of the circle and *Be Bullied.*'

I'm stuck. I walk slowly into the centre of the circle. Some things in school are just unnecessary. I mean there might be a bit of a point in learning English and you might use some Maths in shops and stuff but nobody needs to go into a circle and pretend to be bullied. When you come to think of it being forced to stand in front of your whole class and do something you don't want to do is bullying. It's just that because teachers do it they call it education.

I stand in the centre of the circle. I can hear the morons at the back muttering 'pervert' under their breath. It's a bit of a record for them, managing to remember a word that long. Johns tries to get the group to be 'absolutely silent'. This takes him a while because my class thinks 'absolutely silent' means not shouting. Then when he's finally got them quiet he realizes that about three people are eating so they all have to go and put their food away. Then he hears the tinny sound of someone listening to her mp3 player. It's bound to be a girl because they can hide the lead in their hair. Then he tries to confiscate the mp3 player but she won't give it to him so in the end he backs down and says she can keep it this once. And by the time he's done that everyone has started talking again and he's got to try and shut everybody up all over again.

All this time I'm standing in the centre of the circle with everyone looking at me. You think that standing up is the easiest thing in the world, right? You've been doing it since you were a baby so you can't do it wrong. But it's weird. When you're standing up in front of a group of people for a bit you start to think that you can't even stand up properly. Your legs feel wrong and you don't know what to do with your hands. They start to feel really big and clumsy. And some girls always start laughing at you. And then you start to worry that you're going red. And then if you start worrying about going red, even if you weren't going red before, you're bound to go red then. And then you think that your flies are undone but you can't do anything about it because if you reach down to check someone might see and get the wrong idea and that's no fun any time – but today, when everybody already thinks I'm some kind of weird pervert, it would be a disaster.

So, finally, after Johns gets into a big enough stress, the class shuts up. 'People, people. Mickey, will now present his piece. People, I give you *Monologue of a Victim* by Mickey Sharp.'

I don't say anything. I've got nothing to say. There's a few giggles from the class. I just stand there looking bored. The class whisper a bit and then they shut up. They know he's going to have a go at me and they don't want to miss it. There's one thing that will shut up every class in our school and that's to watch somebody else get shouted at. It's the only fun most of them get. The silence carries on. You can feel the class getting restless. It's like they're thinking, OK. Come on. Have a go at him. He hasn't done any work.

And the silence goes on. And then it stops when Johns starts clapping.

'Brilliant,' he says. 'Mickey has encapsulated in pure drama the essential suffering of the victim. The bullied who is denied a voice. You fortunate people have just witnessed a perfect dramatic moment.'

The bell goes. Everybody heads off to lunch.

I'll never understand school. You work like anything to produce a piece of work and all that happens is that you get moaned at about the number of spelling mistakes or leaving out the full stops. You do nothing and somebody tells you you're brilliant. I'm going to try doing nothing more often.

I've got to find Justine Bird. She's the person who could lead me to the number nine of the Blondel

Babes and give me a chance of cracking this case. I've got to find her quickly though. The final is tomorrow and I've still got no idea where the trophy is, never mind how to get it back.

I start wandering round the school. First, I check the lunch queue. She's not there. Then, I check the canteen. She's not there. I walk round the school about three times looking for her but I don't have any luck. It's really strange looking for a Year Seven kid when you're in Year Nine. You have to spend the whole time looking down because most of them are really tiny and you never normally notice them. You see people in Year Nine because you know them and you keep an eye on the people in Year Ten and Eleven just in case one of them decides to hit you, but nobody in Year Seven is ever going to hit you so you forget they're there unless you stand on one by mistake or something.

In the end, I spot a couple of girls who might be in Year Seven and ask them if they know her. They say she might be in the library. And she is. She's not reading a book or anything. She's just sitting with another little kid talking. Loads of little kids go up to the library at lunchtime, not because they want to read or anything but to keep out of the way of all the nutters in our school who spend most lunchtimes hassling them. We did this thing in Science once about the food chain. Basically, it just means that small things get eaten by medium things that get eaten by big things. Wycherley, our science teacher, went on about how this showed how wonderful nature is and about how all creatures are dependent on each other for survival. I reckon it shows that life is much more fun if you're a big thing.

Schools are like food chains except that instead of big kids eating little kids they hit them. There's nothing the little kids can do about it, except go and hide in the library because there's a teacher there. You're supposed to be silent in our school library but nobody is. They never read any books either, they just get *The Guinness Book of Records* out and look at all the pictures of weirdos.

I go over to Justine and her friend. They see me coming and put their heads down.

'Hi,' I say.

They both start giggling.

'You're Justine Bird, right?'

They look at each other and start giggling some more.

'You're in the Blondel Babes, yeah?'

More giggling. Then they nudge each other. Then some more giggling.

'You're a good team. It's the final tomorrow, isn't it? I'm gonna come and watch. I wasn't always sure about girls' football but I really think your team are good.'

They stop giggling. They look at each other. They start giggling again. This is getting to be a right pain.

'Yeah, I was just wondering what the name of your centre forward is, you know, your number nine, because she's really good and I … er … I just wondered what her name was?'

They aren't giggling any more. Now they're having hysterics.

'What?' I ask.

They start shaking. They've both gone all red.

'Hey,' I say. 'Could you stop laughing for a second? One second. Please.'

They keep laughing. One of them looks like she's laughing so much she's going to stop breathing in a second. That would be just my luck. I come over to ask one simple question and I end up killing a Year Seven girl. The thing is that even if one of them did die the other one would laugh some more.

I try and figure out how to shut them up. Slapping is supposed to be good but if I slapped a Year Seven in the library, I'd be outside Walton's office and having my head yelled off before you could say 'expelled'. But the thought of Walton gives me an idea.

I look over their heads and make my face go all frightened. Then I say, 'Hello, Mr Walton.'

It's exactly like when you turn off a tap. As soon as they hear the name 'Walton' they stop giggling.

'Mr Walton,' I carry on, still looking over their heads. 'Justine was just telling me the name of the number nine in her football team. Weren't you, Justine?' Justine nods. She doesn't even dare turn round.

Justine mumbles the name but she says it so quietly I don't get it.

'Who?' I demand. I've got to get the answer out quick before they start giggling again.

'Deirdre Dean,' she says.

'Which class is she in?'

'She doesn't go to this school. She's at St Veronica's.'

My heart sinks. St Veronica's is an all-girls school. Justine turns round and sees that Walton isn't there. She nudges her friend. She turns round and sees Walton isn't there. There's no prizes for guessing what happens next. They both start giggling.

Still, I've got what I want so I walk off trying to work out how I'm going to get to talk to a girl in a girls' school when I don't even know what she looks like. As for why those Year Seven girls were laughing. Don't ask me. There are some questions which even the best detective in the world couldn't answer, and why Year Seven girls are always laughing is one of those.

CHAPTER 12

I get my bike, slip out of the school gates and head for St Veronica's. I've got no option. The final is tomorrow and all I've got is one piece of pink strip to show for all my investigations. I'm going to get into more trouble than you can possibly imagine on Monday when Newman catches on that I've bunked Friday afternoon and gets the news to Walton. Two detentions and then truanting as well. Still, they can't catch me until Monday and by then I'll have either solved the case or not and I'll have some spare time to fit in all the detentions and tellings off. It's not like I don't plan my schedule.

By the time I get down to St Veronica's lunchtime is over. At least I figure it must be over because there isn't anybody out on the playground. So, now what do I do? I kind of rushed down here without thinking of any kind of plan. It was just my only lead so I decided that I had to follow it. Now I'm here it feels more like a dead end. The best idea I can think of is to wait outside until school ends and ask little kids who come out to tell me who Deirdre Dean is so I can talk to her. The trouble is that even I can see that the plan is filled with great big holes. I mean, I might not ask any girls who know her. She might have gone before anyone can tell me. Her mum or dad might be waiting outside the school gate to give her a lift so I couldn't talk to her. Or some teacher might see a strange boy pestering Year Seven girls and ring the police and the last thing I want is to be meeting the police again under those unfavourable circumstances. They might get the wrong idea.

I take a look at the school in the hope that it will give me an idea. It's not like our school. It's old and it doesn't look like it's going to fall down tomorrow. It's made out of bricks. Our school looks like it's made out of cardboard. The walls are so pathetic inside that you can smash your hand through them if you hit them hard enough. It's the morons at the back's favourite hobby – our tutor room looks like someone's blasted a machine gun at the back wall. If you try to open a window the teachers have a heart attack because last year a sheet of glass fell out and smashed on Andy Phipps' head in Year Ten when he was opening one. His parents came up to see Walton and said they were going to sue the school but I don't know whether they did. He won the prize for best pupil in his year group that year. Only teachers are allowed to open windows now and they do it really carefully. I reckon that it shows what adults really think of kids. They always say how school's really important and stuff and how much they care and then they put you in places that are falling down. See the places where adults work like offices or shops. They're always really smart and painted properly and stuff. Their windows don't fall out on your head.

But St Veronica's is different. It looks like it'll stay up but all the bricks are really dirty and it looks more black than red which is what bricks should look like. It would be fairly depressing going to school there if you ask me – a bit like going into a haunted house or something.

And then out of nothing I get an idea. It's risky and it probably won't work but it's all I've got. I lock my bike to the railings and walk into St Veronica's. I go to the front door, which has a sign on it saying only staff and visitors enter through this door. I push it. It's locked. There's an intercom thing. I press it. There's a buzz and then a woman's voice says.

'Yes?'

'Hello, I've brought a message for Deidre Dean in Year Seven. I'm her brother.'

That's the plan.

'Push the door now, please.'

There's another buzz. I push the door. I'm in. There's an office with a window. As I come through the door, a woman sticks her head out.

'Welcome to St Veronica's,' she says. 'Can I be of any assistance?' She's got this red dress on and she smiles at me. She's nothing like the secretary at our school who growls at you.

'Yes,' I say. 'I'm Deidre Dean's brother in Year Seven and I've got a message for her.'

'OK,' she says. 'Write it down and I'll get it sent to her class for you.' She pushes a piece of paper towards me. This is no good. I need to see her.

'My mum asked me to tell it to her. It's very important and, er, personal.'

'She is in class,' says the secretary. 'We don't like disturbing pupils in class. Are you sure it couldn't be written down?'

'No,' I say. For the first time her face begins to show a little bit of suspicion. I can't let her start to think that there's something dodgy about me or I'll be in real trouble. I don't even know if the front door will open if I need to run. She might have to buzz the door to let you out.

'Well, I'm not sure. This is my first week, you see. I'm not sure of the procedure. I'll just check with Mrs Macavady to see if it's all right.'

I don't know who Mrs Macavady is but I get the

distinct feeling that if she gets down here I might find myself in trouble. She might be a teacher and teachers are always going to be more difficult to fool. They never give you the benefit of the doubt, which in this case would be fair enough. She picks up the phone on her desk. I need to stop her ringing.

'We've got family problems,' I say, 'that's why my mum couldn't come herself.' I put my face in my hands like I'm crying. Then I move my shoulders up and down.

'Oh, you poor boy,' she says. I hear her put the phone down. I move one finger into my ear and push down really hard on the spot. Two seconds later there's water pouring out of my eyes.

'Oh dear. I'll get her for you straightaway.'

'Thanks,' I say and then I do a big sniff.

'What class is she in?'

'I don't know. I just know she's in Year Seven.' And then I do a big snuffle.

'Don't worry, don't worry,' says the secretary. 'I can find her on the computer. Dean … Deidre …' I hear some tapping. 'There we are. 7B. At the moment they are in … ' I hear some more tapping. ' … room 23. I'll just go and get her. Try to pull yourself together whilst I'm gone. You're her big brother. You don't want to upset her, do you?'

'Miss,' I say, 'is there anywhere I can sit and wait

where people can't see me? I don't want girls … I mean people to see me, you know, er … you know.'

'Oh, how insensitive of me,' she says. 'Of course you wouldn't want to be sitting in public view. Go into that room over there. It's where we keep the kettle for making our coffee. There might be some biscuits in the tin if you want one.'

She rushes off to get Deidre and I slip quickly into the room. It's tiny but it's out of sight. It's got a glass door but it's that kind of lumpy glass they have in toilet windows so you can't see through it very well. I shut the door and spit on my hands. Then I wipe the spit down both my cheeks. It's not the most fun thing to do in the world but I figure it'll make me look like I've just stopped crying.

After I've done that I wash my hands in the little sink and open the tin marked BISCUITS. It's got some bourbons and some custard creams and three jammy dodgers. I start to eat. After all, I missed lunch. I can't believe how nice this woman has been to me. Nobody would ever be that nice to you at our school. Even the school nurse who's supposed to be caring just sends you straight back to class unless you're visibly bleeding. One kid in Year Seven had appendicitis and she said, 'Get back to class, Morrissey. You're not in school enough to be ill.' He won the prize for best pupil in his year.

I'm just on my third biscuit when I suddenly tumble to the fact that there's a big hole in my plan. What if Deidre Dean doesn't have a brother? It's so obvious that I can't believe I've missed it. If she doesn't have a brother and a big brother at that then she's going to tell the secretary right away. The secretary's going to realize she's been conned, alert the Head and they're going to be running along the corridor to get to this room and there's only one exit. There's nowhere to run. I think about trusting my luck and betting on her having a brother and then I think about how my luck's been going lately. I decide I can't risk it.

I chuck a couple of jammy dodgers into my mouth and move over to the door but it's too late. Even through the wobbly glass you can still see if someone's coming or not. And someone is coming. I sit down again. The door opens. It's the secretary.

'I've got Deidre with me,' she says. 'I'll leave you here in private to have your little talk. Just come out when you're ready. I hope the news isn't too bad.'

'Thank you,' I tell her. Well, I mean to say thank you but my mouth is full of jammy dodger and they get a bit sticky and so I say, 'Thlet yuk' or something like it.

The secretary goes out and Deidre walks in. She's got this horrible brown uniform on that they have at St Veronica's and she looks nervous. One glance at me and she stops looking nervous and starts looking amazed.

'You're not my brother,' she says, like it was news to me.

'I know,' I say, 'but if you want to stay out of trouble you'd better listen to me and fast.' Well, actually that's what I mean to say but I haven't quite managed to get the jammy dodgers down properly and instead I make a few strange noises and some crumbs fly out of my mouth. One of them lands on her cheek.

'Eeeugh,' she squeaks.

'Sorry,' I tell her. I don't mean to say sorry. I've decided that I've got to be tough with her but it's one of those things that you just can't help saying when you spit jammy dodger in somebody's face.

'She said you were my brother.'

With a massive swallow I manage to get rid of the remains of the jammy dodger and I put on my tough face. It's time to get this interrogation going properly.

'Well I ain't.' And with a flourish, I pull out the piece of pink football shirt from my pocket. 'Why don't you stop worrying about your brother and start talking about this?'

I slam the piece of pink football shirt onto the table in front of her.

'What have you done with him?' she says.

'Who?' I say. She isn't even looking at the piece of football shirt.

'My brother.'

'What?'

'Someone says my brother's here to see me and then I come in here and all there is is you. You're not my brother so what have you done with him?'

'Nothing.'

'Well, where is he then?'

'I don't know.'

'What do you mean you don't know?'

This interrogation isn't going too well at all. She's the one who's asking all the questions when she's supposed to be giving all the answers. I try to swap the positions round a bit.

'Look, I don't know anything about your brother. I want to know what you know about this piece of cloth.'

'Where's my brother?'

'What do you know about the theft of the Georgina Best Memorial Trophy from the headquarters of the Amazons football club?'

'Where's my brother?'

'This piece of cloth was found at the scene of the crime. It is exactly the same size as a piece of cloth which is missing from the number-nine shirt of the Blondel Babes. You wear the number-nine shirt of the

Blondel Babes. You need to explain what you were doing in the Amazons' changing room at the time when the trophy was taken.'

'Where's my brother?'

'Where's the trophy?'

'My brother.'

'The trophy.'

'My brother.'

The door opens. A woman stands there. It isn't the nice secretary. It's a teacher. I just know she's a teacher. She's got that kind of face. Angry.

'What on earth is going on here?' she yells.

'Mrs Macavady,' says Deidre. 'This boy has kidnapped my brother.'

There's no doubt about it. This is not a good situation to be in. There's one way out and it's through the door that Mrs Macavady is blocking. She's a large woman. I can't see much of a gap.

'And he spat biscuit in my face,' adds Deidre.

'I said sorry,' I point out.

'Where's my brother?' Deidre demands.

'Deidre Dean. Be quiet.' shouts Mrs Macavady. 'Now young man. Who are you? What are you doing in my school? Where is this girl's brother? And why are you spitting biscuit in her face?'

You wouldn't think it, but I was the one who'd figured on asking all the questions. The room goes quiet. Deidre stares at me. Mrs Macavady stares at me. Over Mrs Macavady's shoulder I can see the secretary staring at me.

I smile at them. They don't smile back.

'It was only a tiny bit of biscuit and …' I begin.

'Forget the biscuit,' shouts Mrs Macavady. 'The biscuit is a red herring.'

God knows what she means. Herrings are fish and I've never eaten a fish biscuit, but you can get all sorts of weird stuff in the supermarket these days. Anyway, I get the idea she wants me to shut up about biscuit. The trouble is that there are three other questions to deal with. And they're a bit harder. It's like when you do tests in school and you do the first three or four and you think this is OK, I'm going to do all right on this test, maybe I did listen in class after all. And then you get to about question ten and they start getting harder and by the time you've got to question fifteen they might as well be in another language. In French they actually are in another language, which is even more unfair.

'I'm waiting,' says Mrs Macavady.

My mind is a blank. I could tell her the truth. She wouldn't believe it. The story sounds fairly unlikely to begin with and all I've got to back it up is one tiny piece of pink football shirt. The truth would get me nowhere.

'Miss Chappell,' Mrs Macavady says to the secretary. 'I believe we may have to dial 999.'

I need something fast. Think, think, think.

'I am her brother.'

'I beg your pardon,' says Mrs Macavady.

'No, you're not,' says Deidre.

'I wish I'd taken the job at the hospital,' says Miss Chappell.

'Yes, I am,' I say. 'She's just being stupid because we had an argument. You heard us and now she's trying to get me into trouble. I'm her brother.'

'He isn't, Miss,' screams Deidre.

For the first time Mrs Macavady looks a bit worried. She looks at Deidre and then at me and then at Deidre again. She doesn't know who to believe. If I can just make her a little less certain I may just be able to get myself out of here.

'Deidre,' I say, 'it's time to stop being silly. I know you're upset because I came to tell you that mum says you've got to come straight home because we've got to go up to Manchester tonight because grandad isn't very well and that means you'll miss tomorrow's football match but you're not going to change things by making up silly stories, are you? Is she?' I appeal to Mrs Macavady for support.

Deidre stares at me with her mouth opening and shutting like a goldfish. Mrs Macavady looks at Deidre and her face says that she thinks Deidre's the one not telling the truth.

'I'm sorry about this,' I say, 'but I'd better go. Mum told me to come straight back. Mind you come straight back after school now, Deidre.'

I move towards the door and smile apologetically at Mrs Macavady. She's still in the way but I can see in her face that she'll let me go. Mickey Sharp does it again.

'Miss, he's not my brother and I can prove it.'

Suddenly the body in the door is rock solid again. I look at Deidre. She's jammed her hand into a pocket and pulled out a purse. She fumbles it open and pulls out a picture. She whacks the picture down on the table.

'Miss, that's me and my mum and dad and my brother on holiday last year.'

I can't stop my face. It panics. Faces betray you like that just when you think you're doing so well. Try asking a girl out. No matter how cool you look when you practise in the mirror, your face always lets you down when it comes to the real thing.

Deidre points at the picture. Mrs Macavady looks at the picture. Miss Chappell peers at the picture over her shoulder. I stare at the picture and keep staring. I've seen that face before. The boy in the picture is … Kyle Kingston!

'That's not your brother,' I tell Deidre. 'That's …'

'Miss, that is my brother. That's Eric, my brother. We're on holiday in the Canary Islands. My mum got food poisoning. Honest, Miss. Don't believe him.'

And then the tears start. You might as well give up once a girl starts crying. It's their ultimate weapon. There's nothing you can do against it. The tears suddenly work their magic on Miss Chappell. She pushes past Mrs Macavady, who gives her a nasty look, and goes to put her arm round Deidre. 'There, there, dear. Whoever your brother is and wherever he is, I'm sure everything is going to be fine.'

Miss Chappell seems to have lost the plot a bit. The mention of her brother being in danger means that Deidre lets out a horrible scream. It's the sort of scream little girls have. You wouldn't believe it to look at them, being so little, but when they scream you're surprised every piece of glass in the room doesn't break. They sure pack some power. Mrs Macavady doesn't look anywhere near as sympathetic as Miss Chappell. In fact, she doesn't look sympathetic at all. She's probably seen more girls cry than the woman who sells the pregnancy tests at Boots. But the scream gets to her. I'm watching her and it's like you can see it going through her ears and into her brain. Her face scrunches up like someone's just stood on her head.

'Deidre,' she snaps.

Another scream starts.

'Deidre. Be quiet,' and she moves into the room and grabs Deidre's hand. Hard. You know when they show a penalty in football in slow motion from behind the goal. It's like that. The doorway's like the net and Mrs Macavady's like the goalkeeper. And she's moved early and she's gone the wrong way. All I need to do to score is to go through the gap she's left. I throw myself towards the door, catch my foot on the table, twist round, bounce off the side of the door, avoiding the despairing grab of Mrs Macavady's hands and I slam into the back of the corridor. Goal.

There isn't a crowd and I don't get a cheer. Instead all I can hear behind me is someone yelling, 'Stop.' But I'm through now and the main door isn't far away. I run towards it. Will it open? I pull. It moves. I'm through. With one quick glance back at the despairing faces of the defenders (Mrs Macavady, Miss Chappell and Deidre Dean), I slam the door behind me, leap into the playground, grab my bike and ride and ride and ride.

CHAPTER 13

Kyle Kingston is Eric Dean. Eric Dean is Kyle Kingston. Why?

I get far enough away from the school, buy a coke and a packet of crisps, sit down on a wall and this question bangs away inside my head. It's like when the Maths teacher puts some shape on the board and says now demonstrate why lines AB and lines XY are the same length. And you look at lines AB and XY and they look exactly the same length but you know that just writing down, 'I could tell by looking' isn't going to get you a big tick. There's got to be more to it than that. There's got to be a reason. And I don't know what it is.

Which people change their names? Women who get married (except my sister says she won't), some pop stars, especially rappers (rappers are all called things like DJ Fresh and Big Hard Kool Guy – I bet their real names are things like Leonard and Bernard), and criminals. Kyle's not a woman or a pop star so that makes him a criminal. He had access to Deidre's shirt. He had access to the changing room of the Amazons. He could have stolen the trophy. He must have stolen the trophy. He must be guilty.

But why?

I've seen these detectives on the TV and when they're trying to see if someone did the crime they have to come up with two things. The first is opportunity. That means, if they were able to do the crime. You can't have opportunity if you were somewhere else at the time, for example, if you were in detention being watched by your Head of Year when someone sets the fire alarm off it can't be you. But the other thing you need is motive. Motive is the reason for doing the crime. And I can't figure it out. To help his little sister win a trophy? I don't buy that. The Kyle Kingston I met was so into himself that I couldn't see him doing something that would make anybody else happy. If he did it, it would be so something good could happen to him. And I can't see what that could be.

So, maybe he isn't guilty after all.

There's only one way to find out and that's to go and find him, ask him a few tough questions and see if he starts to sweat.

Unfortunately, I don't know where he lives. I could go back to St Veronica's and follow his sister home and find out but that would be a bit of a risk. If she or

Mrs Macavady saw me hanging around then I could have the police on my tail.

So, I figure that my only hope is to zoom down to the Amazons' pitch to see if he's there. Schools will be finishing pretty soon and I might be lucky and bang into him. It doesn't sound much of a plan to me but it's the only idea I've got in my head and the time to solve this case is disappearing as fast as the morons at the back's brain cells. I've got to do something.

I take my time riding down there. It's a bit of a distance and my legs have done a fair bit of running and riding already. I'm not a huge fan of exercise but walking's boring, the bus is slower than walking and I'm not old enough for a car so pedal power's the only option I've got.

I don't see anything when I get there, just an old guy taking his dog for a walk and a couple of kids I don't recognize taking penalties at another kid. They both score every time; the goalie won't dive because he's got a new tracksuit on and he doesn't want to mess up his labels. I head over to the Amazons' changing rooms. Nobody's around. I try the door. It's locked. I stick my head against the mesh that guards the window and try to look through but I can't see anything because the window behind it is so dirty. I try and fit my hand through the mesh to wipe the window to see if I can get any kind of a look in. Not because I expect to see anything but because as soon as I give up here I'm going to have to admit to myself that I'm out of ideas and that the whole case has beaten me. And that's not a feeling I want.

'And so hopeless detective Mickey Sharp has failed to save the Amazons football club by finding the missing trophy and instead returns to the scene of the crime and attempts to break in himself. Quite a remarkable turnaround in this case.'

I recognize the voice and I recognize the lousy way of talking.

'Shut up, Clive,' I say. 'And I'm not trying to break in. Somebody has already done that.'

'Sharp demonstrates his already well-known tactic of stating the obvious,' continues Clive's voice behind me. 'What do you think of his performance, Trevor?'

'He's got to be disappointed,' says another voice. 'His whole approach has lacked commitment from the start. When you're in these relegation situations, it's important you show a bit of passion and frankly that's been lacking in his display so far. I think he's already resigned himself to dropping out of the detective league. He'll be doing a paper round next season.'

I jag my hand out of the mesh and swing round. Standing next to Clive is a smaller version of him. Presumably Trevor. 'So, what's this – a commentators' club?' I ask.

Clive shakes his head. 'Trevor,' he says, 'is responsible for in-depth match analysis. Every good commentator has to have an expert analyst. It's essential to give the viewer or listener a deeper insight into the game.'

'And he's your little brother,' I point out.

'He's an expert analyst,' says Clive. 'Any personal relationship between us is irrelevant. Isn't it, Trevor?'

'Absolutely, Clive. What matters in the commentator/ analyst relationship is that the individuals function as a team, criticizing the same things, praising the same things and always observing that the referee doesn't have video replays like we do.'

'What video replays?' I ask.

'Trevor is looking to the future,' says Clive. 'One day we will have video replays.'

'I'm looking for Kyle Kingston. Any idea where he might be?' I don't want to hear any more about the future of Clive and Trevor.

'Sharp is searching for Kyle Kingston,' Clive starts off. 'But I'm afraid that from what this commentator has observed of his detective skills he hasn't got much chance of finding him.'

'Absolutely, Clive,' says Trevor. 'Sharp's way out of his depth here.'

'Do you know where he is?' I ask them saying every word deliberately slowly.

'At the moment this commentator cannot

enlighten the viewer with the information he requires,' says Clive.

'Absolutely, Clive,' says Trevor.

'You mean "no",' I say.

'Absolutely, Clive,' says Trevor.

'My name's not Clive,' I tell Trevor. And then I go. It's beginning to get dark and I've had enough.

CHAPTER 14

There's only one person left. Katie Pierce. I've tried everything I can and she is my final, last and only hope. Having Katie Pierce as your last hope is like finding out that the only person who'll let you copy their French homework is one of the morons at the back. But it's either that or go home and sit in the shed and wait for Phoebe to turn up and kick footballs at my head because I haven't got her stupid trophy back for her. Why do girls need to play football anyway? What was wrong with netball and hockey? Nobody ever stole a hockey trophy.

I feel like my dad says he feels all the time. Old, tired and stressed out. Maybe I'm not cut out for this detective thing after all. All I ever seem to do in this case is make mistakes and mess things up. I've still only got one pink piece of shirt to show for three days' work and I didn't even find that. I drag it out of my pocket and stare at it. Stupid piece of cloth. I throw it on the ground.

At least, I aim to throw it on the ground but I can't even do that right. A bit of wind picks it up and lifts it into the air. It hangs for a second just in front of my face and then floats slowly down and settles on my wrist. I don't know why but I stick it back in my pocket. Maybe all Walton's assemblies about litter are finally getting to me.

I head towards Katie Pierce's house. I found out her address a few weeks ago because of a couple of things which came up in my last case and needed sorting out but I've never actually been there. It's over in the posh area of Hanford where there are trees on the pavement and everybody has about four cars. Katie's dad works in advertising and earns more than a hundred grand a year and they always go somewhere really posh for their holidays. Katie's mum, the school governor, gives us talks on the evils of smoking and writes complaining letters to any teacher who criticizes Katie. You don't need to be Katie's friend to know all this, you just need to be in our classroom because she goes on and on about it. I don't know why her friends put up with it. Well, I do. It's because Katie's scary.

Because it's getting dark, it takes me a bit of time to find Orwell Avenue but I get there in the end. Her house is the biggest in the whole street. Mind you, if Katie was my kid, I'd make sure I bought a big house because with a voice like hers you don't want her too near.

And now what do I do? I wait and I watch. This is the worst thing about being a detective. Waiting. I'm no good at it. I get really impatient just queuing up in our school canteen and when you taste what they give you it makes you wonder why you queued up in the first place. This is worse though because I don't even know why I'm waiting. Well, maybe I do – it's because I haven't got any other idea what to do.

The good thing about this being a really posh road is that I can wait without standing out too much. It's dark and there are loads of trees and so, provided I keep out of the light from the street lamps, I shouldn't attract any attention. That's the problem with being a teenager. If you aren't doing anything adults automatically assume that you are about to do something bad. They call the police on you just for standing around. They can even prosecute you for it. 'Loitering' they call it. They have to give it a fancy name to make it sound worse than it is but all it means is standing around, not doing anything. And Newman, my form teacher, reckons that this is a free country. It might be a free country if you're thirty and going grey. It's a police state if you're fourteen. Some guy with glasses and a face like a ferret was on the news last week going on about curfews. I didn't know what they were but my dad said it meant that children had to be in bed by a certain time every night or the government would take them to court and lock them up. Then he said that he hoped I broke the curfew. All adults hate kids. Don't believe them when they say stuff is for our benefit because it's not.

And then, just when I'm thinking about curfews, round the corner comes Kyle Kingston or Eric Dean or whoever he is. I'm about to step out of the shadows and front up to him all the stuff I've found out but then I stop. If he's going to Katie's then I might be better waiting to see what happens before I give him the third degree.

I push my body hard against the tree and I hear him go past. You always think people can hear your heart beating or your breathing when you're trying to keep out of sight. It's like when you used to play Hide and Seek when you were a kid. Once he's past me I can relax a little. I'm still in the shadows so there's no way he can see me. I watch him as he walks up the drive to Katie's house. Then he bends down and picks something up. Then he chucks something and I hear a couple of taps. I can't quite work out what's going on but then the curtains in one of the rooms upstairs go back and whole load of light shines out and I can see a lot better. A window opens and Katie sticks her head out.

'Eric? Eric? Where are you, Eric?' says Katie.

'Don't call me Eric,' says Kyle.

'Why, Eric, it's your name?'

'I've told you not to call me that. The only people who call me that are my mum and dad and my sister. To the rest of the world I am Kyle Kingston. The Kylester.'

So, Katie knows about Kyle's little secret.

'All right, Kyle,' sighs Katie, 'If you want to deny your name that's not my problem. Is everything going OK?'

'The Big K delivers, Katie. They're still looking for the stolen trophy.'

'Stolen,' says Katie and they both start laughing. I don't get the joke but then I don't fancy sharing a sense of humour with those two anyway.

'Katie,' says Kyle, when they've stopped giggling.

'What?'

'You're beautiful. When you stuck your face out of that window it was like the sun coming out and the Big K is a big fan of the sun.'

I'm so shocked by what Kyle says that I nearly fall over. He's in love with Katie Pierce. He maybe the most arrogant, unpleasant guy I've ever met but I almost feel sorry for him.

'Not this again,' says Katie. 'And keep your voice down. If my mother finds you out here she'll kill you.'

'The Kylester would rather die than be without you.'

'Oh God,' says Katie.

'I wish I was your pet, Katie.'

'I'd have to put you to sleep.'

'I wouldn't mind dying.'

'I wouldn't mind either.'

'Give the Big K the satisfaction of one kiss tonight.'

'Kyle, I've told you. If I win this trophy tomorrow I'll go out with you.'

'Tomorrow is so far away to The Kylester. I need to be treated right. I've played for England Schools.'

'No, you haven't, Kyle. You've never played for England Schools. A girl like me remembers what she's been told.'

'Oh yeah, I forgot I'd told you. Kyle wishes he hadn't sometimes.'

'And Kyle ...'

'Yeah?'

'If I don't win that trophy tomorrow, everybody's going to know about you not playing for England Schools and all the other things you've been making up. Like the fact that you've never had a girlfriend.'

'Ssssh.'

'Well, make sure I win that trophy or I'll tell everybody that and I'll also drop in the fact that you cover yourself in fake tan and your natural hair colour's brown.'

'Katie. How can you say this to The Kylester?'

'I open my lips, babe. Now clear out of here before my mother finds you. Go on. Go.'

Kyle does what he's told. Mind you, most people do what they're told when Katie Pierce is the one doing the telling. He walks off down the avenue. I press myself back against the tree so he can't see me. I wait for a while to make sure Katie's gone away from the window. I'm trying to make sense of what I've been hearing. Kyle's fallen in love with Katie Pierce. Because of that he's told her that he's not really Kyle Kingston but Eric Dean and that he's never played for England Schools and he's never had a girlfriend and loads of other stuff. That's a really dumb thing to do but people do dumb things when they're in love. One of the morons at the back wanted a girl to go out with him so much that he carved her name on his arm with a knife. He got blood poisoning and was in hospital for a week and she still wouldn't go out with him. Anyway, Katie's said she'll go out with Kyle if he helps her win the trophy and then she won't have to be a football coach next year. If he won't help she'll tell everybody what a fraud he is. He must have stolen the trophy to make sure that the Blondel Babes won it because if he'd seen them play he must have known that there was no chance of them winning it by playing football.

It all links together. It's amazing. I've solved the case.

Except I haven't. I still haven't the faintest idea where the trophy is. I know who took it but I don't

126

know what happened to it. And I haven't got any way of finding out. Katie Pierce will deny all knowledge if I ask her. Kyle will do anything to get a date with Katie so he isn't going to help me. If I confront him he'll just deny it and he'll probably hit me too. It's not fair. All this work and I'm so close and I'm not going to solve the case. Phoebe will go mad.

I lean against the tree for five minutes thinking about everything that has happened. There has to be something. Something that I've missed. Something someone's said or someone's done which will lead me to the answer.

Nothing.

I've had enough. I get on my bike and ride home. My mother will probably kill me because I didn't come home for my tea. As I whizz towards our house I notice a few girls hanging around. They're standing outside David's house. They take a quick look at me as I ride up, all look disappointed and turn their heads back to David's house. I try not to feel offended. I get off my bike and wheel it quietly into our back garden and down towards the shed. I want to delay the telling off my mother's going to give me until I've cooled down with a packet of crisps and a Coke.

There's somebody outside the shed. It's David. He doesn't look happy. Come to think of it nobody looks happy when they see me. It's like I smell bad or

127

something. Still, after all the cycling I've been doing today, I probably do.

'Are they still there?' David says.

'Who?' I ask.

'The girls.' He says girls like most people say rats.

'The ones outside your house?'

'Yes.'

'There's three of them.'

'This is all your fault.'

'My fault.' I seem to be getting the blame for everything these days. Even things I haven't got a clue about.

'Yes. They think I'm a pop star and a model and everytime I go outside they start screaming at me, taking pictures and asking for my autograph. They tried to pull my clothes off as well. One of my grey jumpers is ruined and some girl ran off with my guard's cap.'

'It's tough being a celebrity.'

'You don't understand. I'm like a prisoner in my own house.'

'So what? You never go out anyway,' I point out. 'You just stay upstairs playing with your trains.'

'It's not playing. I'm running a network. And that's the worst thing. I can't concentrate on my trains any more. Just knowing they're there makes me lose concentration. There have been so many near misses that I've had to suspend my timetable.'

'David,' I tell him, 'that's what girls do. They distract you. They get into your head and you can't get them out. It happens to all of us. It's perfectly normal.'

'I don't want to be normal,' he says. 'I want you to get rid of them.'

This is the thanks I get. I turn Hanford's biggest social reject into a sex symbol and all he does is moan. I give it one last shot. 'What about the girls you met at the Xanadu? I think one of them might like you.'

'Them. They probably started this rumour. I never want to see any of them again. Do you know they didn't know the difference between a signal box and a level crossing?' And with a disgusted shake of his head he walks off. Then he stops and turns round. 'Oh, and there was a girl here looking for you. She didn't seem very happy.'

'What did she look like?'

'I don't know. They all look the same to me. But she had a football and she said to tell you that you'd better have it by tomorrow or you're going to be history. And she kept saying "period." I've no idea why.'

And with that he goes.

'Where's my cat?'

I look down. Emerging from behind a bush is little Jeremy Thomas. With everything that's been going on I'd forgotten all about him.

'It's been three days and I've heard nothing from you. What kind of detective do you call yourself?'

This is unbelievable. I'm now getting told off by a six-year-old.

'Listen, kid,' I tell him. 'I've got too much to worry about at the moment without having to look for your dumb cat. I'd have told you that I couldn't take your case but you left too quickly.'

'Nonsense,' little Jeremy shakes his head. 'I want my cat back.'

'I haven't got your stupid cat.'

'Well, you should have. I gave you the job of getting my cat back so you should have it back.'

There's no arguing with little kids when they get something into their heads. They stop listening to you. They just say the same thing over and over again. But whatever happens I don't want him to start crying. The last thing I need is to be found at the bottom of our garden with a little kid in tears, especially one who's got glasses with a patch over one eye.

'There's no need to get upset,' I tell him, trying to make my voice sound calm. 'You don't want to cry about this.'

'Cry,' says Jeremy, looking at me like I've just made the dumbest suggestion in the world. 'Cry is the last thing I'll do. I'm going to phone *Watchdog*.'

'What?' I can't believe it. *Watchdog* is this programme for people who want to complain about dodgy companies.

'You said you'd find my cat. And you haven't found it. I'm going to make sure that everybody who watches the telly knows what a rubbish detective you are and then you'll never get a case again.'

And with that he turns his back on me and stomps off down the garden.

Great. I'm now going to be slagged off on national TV as a lousy detective. And, according to David, Phoebe's after me as well. I'm about as popular as Geography homework. I decide to get my last telling off over with and head inside so my mum and dad can abuse me for worrying them sick by not coming home for my tea. If I look sulky they might ground me for a month and then I'll never have to see Phoebe or David or Katie or Kyle or Clive or Trevor again.

CHAPTER 15

Some hope. Just when you want your parents to ground you they don't. They'd been called over to my gran's earlier in the evening because she fell over or something and they weren't back so they didn't know that I'd missed tea. My sister was on the phone when I got back and had been for about the last three hours so she didn't care whether I'd been in or not, which meant that when next door's car alarm wakes me up the next morning I'm free to go out. Typical.

I figure I could hide. I could just ride into town and stay out all day and then nobody would be able to find me and it would all be over before I had to face up to Phoebe. At least then she might have had time to calm down. It seems like a plan. I head into the shower and kick about what I could do with the day. I could catch a movie, hang out round the shops, get a burger. The trouble is that all the time I'm thinking about doing this there's this voice in my head saying, 'Coward, coward, coward'. I try to ignore it. I try to argue with it till my mum bangs on the bathroom door and tells me to stop talking to myself. But I lose. You can win every argument in the world except the ones with the voice inside your head.

I quit the shower, chuck on some clothes and head downstairs. I phone Julie Reece and tell her that David's modelling contract and his pop contract have been cancelled because he's suddenly developed a nasty rash on his face. I offer to put in a good word for her. She tells me she isn't that keen any more, which is a big surprise. I hang up. She'll put the word around for definite and that'll be the end of the girls outside his house. So, at least I've sorted something out even if it was a mess that I made myself. It doesn't make me feel any better and I figure that only one thing is going to. I get on my bike and head for the Blondel Babes' ground where the final is. Admitting that I've blown it isn't going to be any kind of fun but it's the only way to get the voice inside my head to shut up.

I get there just after half past nine and the game kicks off at ten. I throw my bike down and walk towards the pitch. The teams are already there and there are a few mums and dads hanging round the touchline waiting for the action to start. I decide to make a quick getaway once I've given Phoebe the bad news. I don't want some proud dad finding out that I'm the reason his little girl didn't get to play in the final of the Georgina Best Trophy. Dads can get very violent when that sort of thing happens, especially when they've brought their camcorder along specially.

I see Phoebe over on the far side of the pitch. She's watching her team practise shooting. They look pretty good. For eleven-year-olds, a couple have got a decent shot on them. They all seem really up for the game, excited and happy. I'm going to ruin all that. All that energy all ready to explode and it's not going to be able to. I feel a right failure.

Phoebe blows a whistle and the girls stop playing and go over and make a circle around her. It's now or never. I walk over to give them the bad news. Phoebe's got her back to me so she doesn't spot me coming over. When I get there she's giving her final team talk. I decide to wait until she's finished.

'OK, y'all,' she says, 'enjoy yourselves, right. Express yourselves. Keep it tight in the defence and pass and move. Little triangles. Play the game in their half but don't rush and keep calm in front of goal. Now for the team. Goalkeeper, Grace Banks; Defence: Georgia Cohen, Rachael Wilson, Billie Wright and Bella Moore; Midfield: Teresa Finney, Sarah Matthews, Denrah Edwards and Barbie Charlton and Forwards: Tina Lawton and Jacqui Milburn. Substitutes: Paula Bonetti, Jane Charlton, Letitia Shackleton, Wendy Mannion and Natalie Lofthouse. Now let's go, girls.'

It's terrible watching the team get named. All their faces light up. Any second now I'm going to have to make those faces go dark. I cough. Phoebe turns round. She takes one look at my face and knows something is wrong. 'What's the story?' she says bluntly.

I look at the little girls' faces. I look at Phoebe's face. I look at the ground. I try to find the courage to break their hearts. 'Er ...' I say. The courage isn't there. 'It's coming.'

'What?' yells Phoebe. 'What do you mean it's coming? Why isn't it here?'

'My mother's polishing it.' Don't ask me why I say that because I do not know.

'We don't need it clean,' screams Phoebe. 'We need it here.'

'She's a very fussy woman.' Or that.

'She's going to lose us the cup.'

'But it'll be very shiny when you lose it.'

'Mickey, I'm going to ...'

'Excuse me. Is there some kind of problem here?'

We both swing round. Behind us is a big bald man with a silly moustache and behind him is Katie Pierce.

'Oh, hi, Colonel Blat,' says Phoebe. All the violence disappears from her voice and she suddenly sounds friendly. 'No, there's no problem here. Colonel Blat is the Chairman of the Georgina Best Memorial Trophy

Committee, Mickey,' she tells me, in a voice that says smile and look friendly.

I smile at him. He looks as though he's just spotted something unpleasant and looks away. My fake smiles aren't my best. I look as if I'm being electrocuted. You should see my dad's photo albums.

Katie Pierce keeps looking at me. 'Hi, Mickey,' she says with a sweet smile. 'You backing another loser? Story of your life.'

'Right-oh,' says the bald guy. 'Let's see this show on the road. Kick off in five minutes. May the best team win and all that. I've got a fourball this afternoon so let's make it sharpish.'

'Oh, Colonel Blat,' starts Katie and from the way she says his name I know it's going to be dangerous, 'I was just wondering where the trophy is. The Amazons have got to return it, haven't they, before the game starts?'

'Quite right, my dear,' says Blat. 'Thanks for reminding me. I'm getting forgetful in my old age. Well, then, hand it over. Got to have something to present at the end of the game, haven't I? Look a bally fool standing there with my hands empty.'

They both look at Phoebe, who looks at me.

'My mum's cleaning it up,' I say, trying to sound like I believe it. 'It'll be here any minute.'

'Really?' says Katie Pierce. 'I didn't think much got cleaned in your house, Mickey.'

'It'll be here soon, Colonel Blat,' says Phoebe. 'I promise.'

'But, Colonel Blat,' says Katie, pulling something out of her pocket. 'Doesn't it say in the rules that if the trophy isn't returned in time for the final then the team who hold the trophy is disqualified? Look it says it here under Rule 18, section 3, subsection 4, paragraph D. I've underlined it for you.'

'You seem very well prepared,' I point out. 'It's like you knew the trophy wasn't going to show up.'

'Mickey,' she says looking shocked. 'A good manager is always prepared for every eventuality. I hope you're not suggesting that I've done something bad. That would upset me. I might cry.'

Cry? Katie Pierce couldn't cry if she tried. Well, not properly anyway. Not like she was really sad or anything.

'Sir,' says the bald guy. 'You should be ashamed of yourself. A man who impugns the reputation of a lady should be horsewhipped. Where are the standards of decency in the young men of today? And we wonder that we lost the empire.'

Phoebe stares at me like she'll do the horsewhipping for him. I don't know what horsewhipping is but it doesn't sound much fun.

'Thank you,' says Katie to the bald man. 'I'm not used to boys and their rough ways.'

Katie Pierce not used to boys. That's like saying hamsters aren't used to wheels.

'Don't mention it, my dear. The day Colonel Archibald Blat, MC, DSO with bar, can't defend an innocent young thing like yourself will be a very sorry state of affairs. Now on the subject of this trophy …'

I know I've blown it. He's gone completely over to her side. He's going to award the game to her.

'Dashed awkward when you come to think of it. No trophy but two teams and a crowd. Seems that if this young man's word can be trusted and the trophy will be along in a jiffy, the best thing to do is to play the game anyway on the expectation that the trophy will turn up. If this young man can't be trusted and the trophy isn't here, then whatever the score, the victors will be the Blondel Babes. That's settled then? Let's get started.'

'But the rules,' says Katie, getting into stress. 'Rule 18, section 4, subsection …'

'Quite right,' says the bald guy, 'but I think if you check Rule 41, section 2, subsection 6, paragraph G it says that, "Under exceptional circumstances, the Chairman may override one or more rules in the interests of the tournament." Wrote the rules myself, you see. Never forget a rule, that's what a life in the army teaches you. Now a final without a trophy – I'd say that was an exceptional circumstance, wouldn't you?'

And without waiting for a reply, he marches off.

Katie looks at me.

'Well Mickey, I hope your mother gets here soon. Though why she needs so much time to clean a black trophy is a mystery to me. You wouldn't have thought that it would show the dirt, would you? Unless of course she hasn't got it. We'll all be waiting to see, Mickey.' And she smiles that sweet but deadly smile she's got and slowly slinks off towards the Blondel Babes.

CHAPTER 16

'I don't like this, Mickey,' says Phoebe. 'I don't like this one bit. Everybody seems to know what's going on but me and if I find out that you've been helping the opposition then I'm gonna be kicking you to the kerb, boy. Literally.'

'It's not me that's been playing with the opposition, it's …'

'AND NOW WELCOME TO THE FINAL OF THE GEORGINA BEST MEMORIAL TROPHY. WE'RE HERE AT THE BLONDEL BABES STADIUM. THE SUN IS OUT, THE SKY IS BLUE. THE PLAYING SURFACE IS PERFECT APART FROM THE REMAINS OF A CAMPFIRE HALFWAY DOWN THE LEFT WING. I'M CLIVE, YOUR COMMENTATOR FOR TODAY'S GAME …'

I don't believe it. Some fool has given Clive a microphone and a PA. Clive isn't going to let an opportunity like this pass by. He's cranked the volume up to maximum and his voice is booming out across the park. The interruption shuts down my talk with Phoebe. She gives me a disappointed shake of the head and runs off to give her team some last-minute advice.

'BESIDE ME, I HAVE TREVOR WHO'S READY WITH SOME IN-DEPTH ANALYSIS. TREVOR, HOW DO YOU SEE THIS GAME GOING?'

'WELL, CLIVE, IT COULD GO EITHER WAY. BOTH TEAMS LIKE TO PLAY FOOTBALL AND IT ONLY TAKES A SECOND TO SCORE A GOAL.'

There's a loud blast on a whistle and the game kicks off.

There's nothing to do now but watch and hope for a miracle. I've tried every angle I can think of and I've got nothing. I wander over to the touchline and join the crowd. By crowd I mean about twelve dads, two mums, fifteen younger brothers and sisters and four dogs.

'MOORE THROUGH TO CHARLTON. SMART PASS TO MATTHEWS. SHE BEATS ONE. SHE BEATS TWO. SHE'S GOT TO THE BYLINE. THE CROSS COMES IN. LAWTON RISES LIKE WELL-MADE BREAD. SHE MEETS THE BALL WITH A CRASHING HEADER. ONE-NIL TO THE AMAZONS. WHAT A

GOAL! WHAT A START! WHAT ARE YOUR THOUGHTS, TREVOR?'

'WELL, CLIVE. THE EARLY GOAL. BUT THE DEFENCE WILL BE VERY DISAPPOINTED WITH THAT. THE MARKING WAS … OW! THAT MICROPHONE JUST GAVE ME AN ELECTRIC SHOCK.'

The Amazons celebrate. Their dads cheer. The Blondel Babes look depressed. Their dads all swear at the referee and claim it was offside. Two dogs invade the pitch. There's only four minutes gone.

By half-time, it's 3–0. The Amazons are all over the Blondel Babes. The Blondel Babes' dads are swearing at everyone. The girls look like they want to go home. The only happy member of the Blondel Babes team is their manager, Katie Pierce, who watches the game with a smug smile on her face. Every goal that goes in makes her smile even more. I reckon she'd rather win by cheating than by her team actually scoring more goals than the opposition. It gives her a thrill.

The Amazons on the other hand all look happy. Phoebe's got carried away by the superb performance of her own team and forgotten about the cup for a while. The team all look really pleased. If it's possible, I feel even worse.

But then Phoebe remembers about the cup. She looks at me with a question in her eyes. I shrug. She looks disgusted and turns away. I've let her down, I've let the team down and I've let Katie Pierce win. All that I've got left to do on this case is wait to see The Blondel Babes crowned champions no matter how many goals they let in and then get yelled at by Phoebe. What a way to spend your weekend. I'd rather be round my gran's. I'd rather be in detention. I'd rather be gardening with my dad. I'd rather be anything but this.

'AND NOW,' booms out Clive, 'THE TEAMS RUN OUT ONTO THE PITCH FOR THE SECOND HALF. AND THE QUESTION ON EVERYBODY'S LIPS IS CAN THE BLONDEL BABES TURN IT ROUND? WHAT'S YOUR VIEW, TREVOR?'

'I'M GOING NOWHERE NEAR THAT MICROPHONE. IT'S A DEATH TRAP.'

'COME ON, TREVOR. THE CROWD REQUIRES SOME IN-DEPTH ANALYSIS.'

'I DON'T CARE.'

'TREVOR.'

'NO.'

'TREVOR, PLEASE.'

'NO.'

'TREVOR.'

'OW. STOP HITTING ME.'

'YOUR VIEWS, TREVOR.'

'MY VIEW IS THAT YOU SHOULD STOP TWISTING MY ARM. OWWW. MY VIEW IS THAT THEY NEED TO REORGANIZE AT THE BACK AND START PASSING TO EACH OTHER AND TRY SHOOTING ONCE IN A WHILE.'

'THANK YOU, TREVOR. AND THE REFEREE BLOWS THE WHISTLE AND WE'RE OFF. AND STRAIGHTAWAY THE BLONDEL BABES GIVE THE BALL AWAY AND THE AMAZONS ARE ON THE ATTACK.'

It's one-way traffic. The Amazons are like Manchester United and the Blondel Babes have given up. I'd feel sorry for them if I didn't know they were going to win the cup anyway.

'COHEN DOWN THE LINE. FINNEY CONTROLS IT ON HER CHEST. SLIDES THE BALL ACROSS TO MILBURN. WHAT A SHOT! THE BALL FLIES THROUGH THE AIR LIKE A FRISBEE WITH AN ENGINE. GOAL!'

Four-nil. The fathers of the Blondel Babes attack the fathers of the Amazons.

'WILSON INTO MOORE. MOORE THROUGH TO EDWARDS. SHE GOES ONE WAY. SHE GOES THE OTHER WAY. SHE GOES A THIRD WAY. SHE GOES BACKWARDS. SHE GIVES IT TO MATTHEWS. MATTHEWS INTO MILBURN. MILBURN TO LAWTON. GOAL!'

Five-nil. The fathers of the Blondel Babes invade the pitch and start shouting at anybody in the team who isn't their daughter. The referee gets a mobile phone out of his pocket and threatens to call the police.

'SOME PEOPLE ARE ON THE PITCH,' booms out Clive. 'THEY WISH IT WAS ALL OVER. IT ISN'T YET.'

The fathers of the Blondel Babes retreat.

'CHARLTON TO EDWARDS TO FINNEY TO MATTHEWS TO LAWTON TO MILBURN. WHAT A MOVE. TO MATTHEWS. SHE AIMS. SHE SHOOTS. GOAL!'

Six-nil. The girls go mad. Their parents go mad. Phoebe jumps up in the air. The dogs start barking. The fathers of the Blondel Babes start hitting each other.

I feel terrible. I shove my hands in my pockets and let my head droop. It's no good being a rubbish detective. I can be rubbish at loads of things, French, Geography, getting on with my parents. The idea of being a detective was to be good at something for once. If I'm just going to be as useless at this as I am at other stuff I might as well forget it.

I feel something in my pocket and pull it out. The little piece of pink football shirt. I blame this for all my problems. If I hadn't found this right at the start of the case then everything would have been different.

Instead of chasing after the wrong things I would have remembered that my job was to find the trophy. But no. I had to discover that Kyle Kingston was a fake, turn David into a rock star and nearly get trapped in a girls' school. None of which was much to do with the job I'd been given. I've messed up.

I look at the little piece of pink. It's funny but even though I've been dragging it round with me for ages I've never looked at it properly. When I found it I was too busy arguing with Kyle and Clive and since then I've just taken it for granted. I look at it properly just once before chucking it away. There's a line of dust on one side of it and I start to rub it clean. It doesn't come off. I rub it a bit harder. It doesn't move. So, I pick at it with my nail and then it starts to move. That's weird, I think. It must be paint or something.

And then suddenly my brain flashes three things into my head at once. Kyle's dirty fingers when he tried to pat my face in the clubhouse. They were dirty even though he'd just had a shower. What doesn't always come off in the shower? Paint. The can I kicked when I walked out of the clubhouse. It wasn't a drink can. It was a paint can. And Kyle and Katie laughing at the idea that the trophy had been stolen. I think I might get the joke now.

The three things bang together and a great big

huge light explodes in my brain and I know where the trophy is.

'How long to go? How long to go?' I yell at the father next to me.

He looks at me like he's going to hit me. And he's got a tattoo on his face.

'Please,' I add quickly.

'Ten minutes,' he says.

Ten minutes. I think about how fast I can ride. Nowhere near that fast. It's going to take me forty minutes to get there and back and I don't have that kind of time. By then, the game will be over, the Amazons will have been disqualified and the Blondel Babes will be the champions.

Bang. I have another idea. Two ideas in two minutes. Has somebody else's brain got into my head? I rush down to where Phoebe is. 'Phoebe,' I say.

'Go away, dumb ass, I'm not talking to you.'

'It's important.'

'Where's your mum and the trophy?'

'Look, I was stalling with that stuff about my mum but I know where it is now. I'm gonna get it.'

'Yeah, yeah, yeah.'

'Honest to God.'

'Don't want to know.'

'Look, I swear to you I know where it is. I can be back here in forty minutes with the trophy.'

For the first time she looks at me.

'What use is that? The game's over in ten.'

'I know, I know. But what happens if the game isn't over in ten.'

'How dumb are you? Football lasts ninety minutes. Then the game's over.'

'But what if it's a draw.'

'We're six-nil up, moron. It isn't going to be a draw.'

'But what if it is?'

'We're going to win. And then lose, thanks to you.'

'Tell me what happens if the game's a draw.'

'All right, already. To get rid of you. If the game's a draw we have half an hour's extra time and then there's a penalty shoot-out.'

'Great,' I tell her. 'So, all you have to do is concede six goals in the next ten minutes. Then play extra time without scoring a goal or letting one in and then win the game on penalties by which time I'll be back with the trophy and you'll be champions. OK?'

'You're mad,' she says. 'Stone crazy. Loopy as a mad thing.'

'I haven't got time for your sweet talk,' I tell her. 'Give me the key to your changing rooms and get your team to let in six goals. There's only nine minutes to go.'

I grab the key and run to my bike. She probably doesn't believe me. But I'm her only hope of keeping her hands on that trophy. I don't know whether she'll help or not. But I do know that she wants to win. Anyway I've got other things to worry about. Like riding faster than I've ever ridden before. I leap onto my bike and make those pedals move.

CHAPTER 17

By the time I get to the Amazons' ground my chest feels like it's about to explode, my heart is beating so fast that it could be the backbeat for a drum'n'bass track and I'm panting like my dad after his jog on New Year's Day. He always says he's going to get fit this year and by the time we go back to school he's put his trainers away for another year.

I force the key into the lock, kick open the door and charge over to the trophy cabinet. Nobody's got round to mending it yet and all the trophies are sitting in the case behind the broken glass. There's loads of them. Which one is it going to be? I look at my watch. Only twenty minutes to go. I haven't got time to find out. There's an old plastic bag lying in the corner. I put my hand through the broken glass front and start pulling out the trophies and packing them into it.

Aaah! Damn. I catch my hand on the edge of the glass as I'm pulling out the last cup and I feel the blood start to run down my wrist. There's no time to

150

do anything about it now. I shove the bag over my shoulder and ride one-handed across the field and on to the road.

Now I need knives. Where am I going to find eleven or so knives immediately? Think, think, think. Our kitchen. The answer hits me and I lose control of my bike for a second. A car beeps me from behind. Our house is halfway between the Amazons' ground and the Blondel Babes' ground. I pedal even faster. I'm going as fast as I can and riding one-handed and that hand's bleeding. I'm all over the road. Cars are beeping at me, drivers are yelling at me but I keep on going.

I get to our house. I throw my bike down. I run like mad to our back door praying that there's nobody in the kitchen. I charge in.

'Mickey,' says my mum, 'where's the fire?'

'I need all your kitchen knives.'

'You're bleeding.'

'It's nothing. Can I have the knives?'

'How on earth did you do that to yourself? It'll need cleaning. Is it deep?'

'Mum, forget about it. Give me the knives.'

'Let me look at it.'

'No. There isn't time.'

'Are you in some kind of trouble?'

'It's too complicated. But this is really important.'

151

'Don't be silly, Mickey. Nothing is more important than that. Now let me look at it.'

'Mum, please. I promise I'll come straight back. I'll be gone half an hour. Please, Mum, please.'

She looks at me. She knows it's important. But she can see me bleeding. And she knows that I could be lying. She's going to say no.

'It's not dangerous?' she says.

'No, Mum. Honest.'

'And you'll be back in half an hour to let me clean that cut?'

'Yes, Mum.' I grab a tea towel and wrap it round my hand.

'And you'll tidy your bedroom?'

'Yes, Mum.'

'Don't ever tell your father.'

She opens the knife drawer. I open the bag. She picks up the kitchen knives and drops them into my bag.

'Thanks, Mum.'

I look at the kitchen clock and the smile that's appeared on my face vanishes. Five minutes. There's no way I'm going to manage that.

'Oh, no.'

'What is it now?' she says.

'I've got be somewhere in five minutes and it's fifteen minutes ride away.'

Mum looks at me. And then she starts to smile. And then she starts to laugh.

'There's nothing funny about it.'

'Oh, Mickey,' she says. 'Get the car keys.'

There are times when your parents amaze you. My mum runs to the car. I've never seen my mum run. I didn't think she could. We get to the car. She pulls open the door and jumps in. I throw myself across the bonnet, drag open the passenger door and I'm in too.

She fires the ignition. The car radio kicks in on a good fast track. The brakes scream as my mum reverses out of our drive.

We get out of our road and zoom down Holmes Street, take a left down Watson Road and pull a right onto the High Street.

And stop. There's traffic piled up and it isn't moving. But time isn't stopping. And there's not much of it left.

'I'm going to have to run for it,' I say. I'll never make it.

'Not so fast,' says my mum.

And she pulls a right into a little side street and starts accelerating down it.

'Mum, it's a dead end,' I tell her. I've seen the sign as we turned in. 'We can't waste time.'

'Mickey, the thing you ought to learn is that just because a sign says you can't do something it doesn't make it impossible. I used to work down here before you were born. And you could get a car through here then.'

'Things have changed since then, Mum,' I tell her.

'Some things haven't,' she slams back. 'Now, keep quiet and let me drive.'

I'm about to have a go back when I'm distracted by something far more important. The road is getting narrower and it's blocked at the far end by a load of boxes.

'Mum,' I scream, 'the road's blocked.'

'We'll have to unblock it then, won't we?'

She pushes down on the accelerator. The track on the radio cranks itself up towards its chorus. The boxes get closer and closer. There's no stopping now. My dad will divorce my mum if she totals the car. The boxes get closer. Electric guitar shrieks through the speakers. I close my eyes.

Bang.

I open my eyes again. The boxes are gone. I flick my eyes to the mirror. They're bouncing about behind us. I flick my eyes back to the road. It's getting narrower and narrower.

My mum keeps going. She's right. It's not a dead end. I can see the opening at the end. But can we reach it? Cars were probably thinner twenty years ago.

There's a terrible screeching sound by my side.

The wing mirror is dragging along the side of the wall. There's blood oozing through the tea towel. My mum keeps going. The gap approaches. The screeching stops and we're out. Right next to the Blondel Babes' ground.

My mum slams on the brakes and the car stops.

'Mum,' I say. I can't say any more.

'Hurry up,' she says.

'Oh, right.'

'And Mickey, I'll be telling your father that someone hit the wing mirror in the supermarket car park. And I think I'll ask Dr Hayes to lower my HRT dosage.'

I don't know what she's going on about and I haven't got time to find out.

I grab the bag with the cups and the knives in and get out of the car.

'I want you back here in fifteen minutes, Mickey. I'll be waiting. Don't make me come after you.'

'Thanks, Mum.'

'Go!'

I sprint towards the pitch, hoping like anything that I'm not too late. I hear Clive's voice booming out, which I figure must be a good sign.

'AND THIS COMMENTATOR HAS NEVER SEEN ANYTHING LIKE THIS GAME. THE AMAZONS, SIX-NIL UP WITH TEN MINUTES TO GO SUDDENLY FALL APART AND

CONCEDE SIX GOALS – ALL OF THEM OWN GOALS INCLUDING ONE ITEM UNIQUE IN FOOTBALL HISTORY WHEN BANKS MANAGED TO SCORE AN OWN GOAL FROM HER OWN GOAL KICK. THERE THEN FOLLOWED A GOALLESS PERIOD OF HALF AN HOUR'S EXTRA TIME IN WHICH THE AMAZONS HAD POSSESSION OF THE BALL ALMOST CONSTANTLY BUT SEEMED DETERMINED NOT TO VENTURE OUTSIDE THEIR OWN HALF OF THE PITCH. WITH THE GAME LEVEL WE REACHED THE DREADED PENALTY SHOOT-OUT. EACH TEAM HAS TAKEN THEIR ALLOTTED FIVE PENALTIES AND THE SCORES ARE DEADLOCKED AT FIVE ALL. SO NOW IT'S SUDDEN DEATH. THE FIRST TEAM TO SCORE WHEN THE OTHER TEAM MISSES OR VICE VERSA WILL BE DECLARED THE WINNERS. I CAN TELL YOU THAT I'M ON THE EDGE OF MY SEAT HERE AND I KNOW MY CO-COMMENTATOR TREVOR WOULD BE TOO IF HE HADN'T HAD TO BE TAKEN TO CASUALTY DURING EXTRA TIME WITH SUSPECTED ELECTRICAL BURNS. AND SO WE AWAIT THE SIXTH PENALTY-TAKER FOR THE AMAZONS.'

I'm all right. I've made it and the game is still going

on. The Amazons are sitting on the pitch around Phoebe who's trying to sort out who's going to take the next penalty.

I force one last surge out of my legs to get to them fast and, without saying anything, turn my bag upside down. Trophies and knives spill out on to the ground.

They all stare at me. Their faces don't look impressed.

'Moron,' yells Phoebe. 'I always knew you were a moron. Don't you understand anything?' She spots my arm. 'You're bleeding. All these knives. You're not a moron. You're a psycho.'

Pervert, moron, psycho. I certainly know how to get myself a good reputation in the neighbourhood. I try to get enough breath to speak.

'Nobody stole your trophy. We thought it was stolen because the cabinet was smashed and it looked like it wasn't there. Kyle Kingston who's really called Eric Dean smashed the cabinet to make it look like it had been stolen. He did it because he's in love with the manager of the Blondel Babes and she said she'd go out with him if he did. But he didn't steal it. He painted it silver and put it back. It was there the whole time. But there's so many trophies that nobody noticed. They just took one look, saw that the black trophy was gone and didn't look any harder. But I don't know which trophy it is. I know that it's one of these, that's all. Everyone grab a knife and start scratching at the trophies until they see some black underneath.'

I say it all so fast that I don't know whether they get it or not. I collapse on to the ground desperate for some air. I've never had such a hectic half hour in my life.

Phoebe is looking at me but not seeing me. It's like she's inside her head playing over what I've just said like she'd taped it on a video. She's got this empty look on her face for about ten seconds and then it snaps back into the real world.

'What are you waiting for?' she tells the team. 'Start scraping.'

They dive for the knives as soon as Phoebe speaks and attack the trophies. It makes a horrible sound.

'CAN WE PLEASE HAVE THE NEXT PENALTY-TAKER FOR THE AMAZONS?' yells Clive out of the tannoy.

The girls all squeak. They are so busy trying to find the trophy that they've forgotten they've got to win it as well.

'Teresa,' snaps Phoebe. 'You go.'

One little girl stands up and walks off.

'The rest of you. Don't watch, just scrape.'

They all start scraping. I'm not scraping but I'm watching them. After a few deep breaths I'm beginning to feel like I'm not going to die in the next thirty seconds and, while this is a good thing in some ways, it's got its bad side. For the first time I start thinking that I might be wrong. What if it isn't there? What a fool I'm going to look. The Amazons might turn nasty. They may only be girls but there's eleven of them (plus subs) and only one of me. I don't like those odds.

'Black,' squeaks an Amazon next to me. 'Look, black.'

She points to her trophy. Everybody charges over to look but I get my head in first. Some black and the letters 'EST' are there. I'm right after all.

'AND FINNEY SENDS THE BALL OVER THE CROSSBAR,' announces Clive.

The Amazons' faces turn from delight to despair. The girl who's holding the trophy drops it.

'What?' I say. I expect a bit more appreciation than that. It's been four days' hard work.

'Don't you get it?' says Phoebe. 'If they score the next penalty they'll have won.'

Oh yeah. I'd missed that because I'd been so relieved that the trophy had turned up.

'AND IT'S UP FOR GRABS NOW,' bellows Clive. 'THE BLONDEL BABES HAVE ONLY TO CONVERT THIS PENALTY TO WIN.'

All the Amazons' eyes are focused on the penalty spot. The trophy is forgotten on the ground. The girl with weird hair from the Blondel Babes walks out.

Georgia, the Amazons' goalkeeper walks out. Teresa Finney comes back. She's crying.

'YOU CAN FEEL THE TENSION,' Clive tells us somewhat unnecessarily. 'BLAIR PUTS THE BALL DOWN. BANKS LOOKS NERVOUS. THE WHISTLE GOES. BLAIR SHOOTS. BANKS DIVES TO HER LEFT. HER FINGERTIPS REACH OUT AND PUSH THE BALL UP AND OVER THE CROSSBAR. SHE'S SAVED IT. BLAIR HAS BLOWN IT.'

The Amazons leap in the air. One of them lands on the trophy.

'Careful,' snaps Phoebe. 'Now get scraping. Sarah, you're up next.'

Somehow all the girls' hands manage to get their knives to reach one trophy.

'AND MATTHEWS PUTS THE BALL DOWN. THE WHISTLE GOES. SHE HITS IT. GOOOOOOAL.'

The Amazons are too busy scraping to cheer. Steadily the silver is coming off revealing more and more black. The trophy is there but they still have to win it. I look over at Katie Pierce on the other side of the pitch. Everybody else looks tense but she's still looking happy. She can't have seen what's been going on.

'AND NOW IT'S DEAN FOR THE BABES,'

Clive tells us as Deidre Dean walks into the area, 'VERSUS BANKS OF THE AMAZONS. IF DEAN DOESN'T SCORE THE TROPHY BELONGS TO THE AMAZONS. HAS DEAN GOT WHAT IT TAKES?'

'She'll score,' says Phoebe. 'She's good. We could be in trouble here. None of the players we've got left have ever taken a penalty before.'

I have an idea. I get up and walk quickly down the touchline. Dean puts the ball down. Banks stands on her line. The crowd goes quiet. I reach the corner flag and start walking towards the goal.

'CAN THE SPECTATOR BEHIND THE GOAL STOP MOVING, PLEASE?' shouts Clive. Everyone looks at me. Including Deirdre Dean. I give her a big smile. She stares at me. The boy who pretended to be her brother. The boy who she thought had kidnapped her brother. Her lower lip begins to tremble. The referee blows the whistle. Everything is silent. Nobody moves for a second. Dean looks at Banks. Banks looks at Dean. Dean glances at me one more time. Then she starts to run towards the ball.

'MISSED,' screams Clive as Dean smashes the shot over the bar. 'IT'S AMAZING, IT'S AWESOME, IT'S THE AMAZONS.'

The Amazons scream and run out to hug Banks. The Babes collapse onto the ground. Deirdre Dean takes one more look at me and then runs very fast in the opposite direction. Katie Pierce keeps smiling. I walk back up the touchline and pick up the trophy.

CHAPTER 18

Colonel Blat appears from nowhere. He's accompanied by Clive who's carrying a microphone. They walk into the centre circle.

'COLONEL BLAT WILL NOW PRESENT THE TROPHY,' announces Clive.

Clive hands the microphone over. Katie Pierce walks into the centre circle. Her smile is getting bigger.

'DASHED STRANGE GAME OF FOOTBALL,' booms Blat. 'AND NOW A DASHED STRANGE PRESENTATION CEREMONY TO FOLLOW BECAUSE I'M AFRAID THAT THERE'S NO TROPHY BECAUSE THAT YOUNG MAN—' He points at me. Everybody turns to look. Katie Pierce shakes her head at me in pretend sadness but the smile is still lurking on the edge of her lips. '—THAT YOUNG MAN LIED TO ME AND SAID THE TROPHY WOULD BE HERE AND IT ISN'T. IF THERE'S ONE THING I HATE IT'S DISHONESTY. IF I HAD MY WAY HE'D BE

PEELING POTATOES TILL CHRISTMAS. BUT THERE WE ARE.'

I start walking towards centre circle.

'SO, THERE'S NOTHING FOR IT BUT TO SAY THAT ACCORDING TO THE RULES …'

Phoebe starts following me towards the centre circle. One by one the Amazons fall in behind her.

'WITH THE AMAZONS HAVING BEEN UNABLE OR UNWILLING TO RETURN THE TROPHY I MUST DECLARE THE WINNERS …'

I hold the trophy high in the air. The crowd gasps. The Amazons cheer. Katie Pierce's mouth drops open so wide you could fit a football through it.

'WHAT?' says Blat. 'YOU'VE GOT THE TROPHY AFTER ALL. WELL, WHY DIDN'T YOU SAY SO?'

I hand it over.

'YOU SAID YOUR MOTHER WAS CLEANING IT. IT DOESN'T SEEM VERY CLEAN TO ME.'

There's still quite a bit of paint on the trophy.

'YOUR MOTHER WOULD NEVER MAKE IT IN THIS MAN'S ARMY.'

I don't respond to the fact that Blat has criticized my mother to the whole crowd. I move to one side giving Katie Pierce a quick wink as I do. Her eyes flash hatred in my direction.

'LADIES AND GENTLEMEN. THE TROPHY HAS NOW APPEARED. I THEREFORE ANNOUNCE THAT THE WINNERS ARE THE AMAZONS.'

Blat hands the trophy to Phoebe. The crowd cheers. The Amazons cheer. I cheer. The Amazons' dads kiss each other. Katie Pierce swears and storms off towards the changing rooms.

The Amazons each take a turn in holding the trophy in the air. Cameras click. Everybody cheers every time a new person holds it up. When they've all had a go they give the trophy to me. I hold it up in the air. All the team cheers. The dads do a conga. Phoebe gives me a kiss. For just a couple of seconds, I feel like a star.

And then almost before I've noticed it's happening, it's stopped. Phoebe takes the trophy out of my hand and passes it to someone else. The Amazons start on a lap of honour. I don't follow them and neither does Phoebe. She looks at me. I look back.

'No win, no fee, Mickey. You remember,' she says.

I don't but I nod anyway.

'So that means win, fee, right.'

I nod again.

'Mickey,' she says, 'you are one amazing guy.'

I feel myself start to go red. And she hasn't even said 'period' yet. She slaps three ten pound notes into my hand. I look down at them. The Queen's face stares out at me. She looks as sick as a parrot. They don't seem much.

'We're square, right.'

I nod.

'You don't seem too pleased,' she says. 'I think that's fair payment.'

'The money's fine,' I tell her. 'It's not that. It's just …'

And then I stop. Whatever words I should say right now aren't coming out.

'Nothing,' I finish.

There's a bit of a pause.

'Nobody back home will believe all this,' she says.

'Back home?'

'Yeah, I fly back tomorrow. Got to bring the Beautiful Game to the dumb hicks in my own country. They still think baseball is the best game in the world. See ya, Mickey. I got to be with my players. If you're ever in LA, look me up.'

And she runs over to the Amazons to finish off their lap of honour. They all run round the field celebrating even though there's only about two people left to watch.

I wander over to the changing rooms and lean against the outside. The Amazons and Phoebe get further and further away. I feel kind of sad. It was

166

like I was part of them for a bit and now I'm not. The record books will remember the Amazons. Nobody will remember me. And LA is an awful long way.

'So, Eric, it was your fault.'

I'm jolted back into life by Katie Pierce's voice behind me.

'Don't call me Eric, Katie.' It's Kyle.

They're behind the changing rooms.

'Everybody will be calling you Eric when I've finished.'

'Please, Katie, how was I to know he'd work it all out just from one piece of pink shirt?'

'Eric, you moron. If you hadn't taken the shirt with you when you went to do the job he would never have had the chance. Why did you do a dumb thing like that?'

'To wipe away any fingerprints.'

'Why not take a normal cloth?'

'Well, Katie. You see, you know how I feel about you.'

'Yes, Eric.'

'And you know that as manager of the Blondel Babes you look after the kit.'

'Yes, Eric.'

'Well, I like to think that it smells of you.'

'It smells of washing powder.'

'Not to The Kylester. To The Kylester it smelt of you.'

'Eric, do you mean to tell me that I've got to manage this team for another whole season because you carried your sister's shirt round with you because it reminded you of me?'

'Yes,' says Eric. 'But let's forget about that now and think about us.'

'Us?' screeches Katie, 'Us! You think that I would ever have gone out with you even if we had won the trophy?'

'You said …'

'I'd go out with Mickey Sharp before I'd go out with you.'

'But you said …'

'Oh, go to hell.'

Katie storms round the corner so fast that I don't get a chance to hide. She stops when she sees me.

'Mickey,' she says.

'Pity about you and Eric,' I tell her. 'You'd have made a lovely couple.'

'Very funny, Mickey.'

'It would have been ideal. You and Eric and Kyle. You know how you like to go out with two boys at once.'

'Laugh it up, Mickey,' she says smiling but her eyes are like ice, 'but you and me both know how much you're going to regret this one day.'

And she turns round and stalks off.

She means it and she doesn't mess around. She might just be right one of these days.

'Ow! Get off! Ow! Aaaargh!'

The scream comes from round the back of the clubhouse. I run around the corner. There's Kyle and there's something on his head.

'Ouch! Help! Help!'

He shakes his head violently and whatever is on his head flies off and lands on the ground. It's a cat. And it's a cat I recognize.

'It just jumped off the roof onto my head. It could have killed me.'

I bend down and look at the cat. It looks back at me. It seems remarkably calm for a creature which only a few seconds ago was trying to kill someone.

'Here, Pudding,' I say. The little black-and-white cat pads over to me and rubs herself against my leg. She starts purring. Maybe little Jeremy Thomas will get his cat back and maybe I won't get reported to *Watchdog* after all.

'The Kylester doesn't know who to kick first – you or the cat,' says Kyle.

I look at Kyle. With all the stuff I've found out about him, I'm not too worried. His threats are like the rest of him. All image. I stare at him. He shakes his head.

'You're not worth it,' he says.

'One thing I don't get,' I say to him. 'Why make up all that stuff about yourself in the first place?'

'Why should I tell you?' he snaps.

'You might as well. Katie's going to tell the whole world on Monday.'

'She won't.'

'Believe me,' I say. 'I know Katie. She will.'

His face kind of crumples as the truth sinks in. 'I wanted to be special,' he says. 'I wanted to be cool. Don't you want to be cool sometimes?'

I decide not to answer that question. I think I am cool sometimes.

'But if you're that good at football why do you need to make the other stuff up?'

He looks really sad.

'It's all made up. I'm not even that good at football. But when we moved to Hanford last year I said I was. And I said I had a long-term knee ligament injury so I couldn't play, so nobody would find out. And so I'd help out with training. And all the girls thought I was really cool. But then I met Katie and she was really nice to me. She said she liked me as a person and so I told her the truth and she used it all to blackmail me into painting the trophy. And now everyone will know about me. We'll have to move house again. I'm going to tell my dad to apply for a new job.'

And he turns round and walks off.

I pick up the cat and walk back round to the front of the clubhouse. The pitch is deserted now. I look at the scene of my triumph. All that's left are empty crisp packets blowing in the breeze and a dog having a pee against a goal post.

I check my hand. It's stopped bleeding. My mum. My mum is sitting outside in the car waiting for me and I've been gone way over fifteen minutes. I dash over and grab the kitchen knives whilst keeping a tight hold on the cat. It's not that easy. The knives are covered in mud. I'll have to wash them and then I'll have to go and buy David a new train or something to make up for all the hassle I've caused him and then I'll have to find little Jeremy Thomas and give him his cat back and then I've promised to tidy my bedroom. I remember what it looked like this morning. I'm not kidding myself. The hardest part of the day is yet to come.

Period.